Midnight Starr

*Midnight
Starr*

the short stories
of

Dorothy Starr

LIBRIS

An *X Libris* Book

First published by X Libris in 1996

A CIP catalogue for this book
is available from the British Library.

ISBN 0 7515 1644 9

Photoset in North Wales by
Derek Doyle & Associates, Mold, Clwyd
Printed and bound in Great Britain by
Clays Ltd, St Ives plc

X Libris
A Division of
Little, Brown and Company (UK)
Brettenham House
Lancaster Place
London WC2E 7EN

Contents

Acknowledgements

'Not Just a Pretty Face' first appeared in *Erotic Stories*, 1992; 'A Pet for Christmas', 'The Man in Black' first appeared in *Forum*, 1992; 'Hand in Glove', 'Sweet Saint Nick' first appeared in *For Women*, 1992; 'Merry Christmas, Mister Lawson', 'Quiet Storm', 'The Old *Uno Due*', 'Stranger Than . . .' first appeared in *Erotic Stories*, 1993; 'Perfecto' first appeared in *Forum*, 1993; 'Studies in Red' first appeared in *Ludus*, 1993; 'Pretty Young Thing' first appeared in *Women on Top*, 1993; 'The Fruits of Learning', 'The Gardener's Boy', 'Finders Keepers', 'Condition Orange', 'Crème de la Crème', 'Thirty-Six Hours' first appeared in *Erotic Stories*, 1994; 'A Thing of Beauty' first appeared in *Loving*, 1994.

Merry Christmas, Mister Lawson

THEY WERE PAYING her triple rate for Christmas Eve. Triple rate and reduced hours . . . and there was no way on earth she was earning it!

The Logicorp Party had been such a sedate affair that the fall-out of canapés, crisps and other assorted mess was minimal. To Nattie Romaine, it almost seemed like cheating to take the extra money, but as the company's Japanese masters had no idea of what constituted a proper seasonal bash in the first place, and were prepared to pay top whack to any person who'd come in and clean up afterwards, how could a poor hard-up student resist? Especially a student who'd nowhere to go on Christmas Eve anyway.

Under normal circumstances, Nattie would've told them to shove it. But circumstances weren't normal this year, and when the domestic supervisor had said, 'Any chance you could do Christmas Eve, Natalia?', Nattie had grimly confirmed she could.

To be alone and sulking tonight was ideal. She'd purposely not gone home for Christmas, so that

1

she and Andy could celebrate together. But now *he* was celebrating with somebody else, and she didn't want to celebrate, full stop. Not with family, not with friends, not with anybody! At the moment, her happiest thoughts came from here; from the necessary part-time cleaning job that topped up her meagre student loan.

Here comes the best bit, she thought, as she pushed open the door to the division head's office – the luxurious acre sized enclosure that was the domain of Mr Jared Michael Lawson, the sexiest thing on two legs that Nattie had seen in a long time!

Very few cleaners got to meet the owners of the offices they tended, but Nattie was lucky. Not only was Mr Lawson fabulously tall, dark and handsome, he was also a workaholic. Nattie's shifts alternated between early mornings, and evenings from seven until nine, but even so Mr Lawson was often at his desk while she worked. There was one particular instance she had special cause to remember: one glorious, blessed-by-heaven dawn . . . But it was no use getting into *that* now, or she wouldn't finish dusting before midnight! This is such a horny-looking office, Nattie decided, throwing her back into her hoovering and wondering if Mr L. ever thought of her as a person. He always seemed too busy even to notice her presence.

The man had beautiful taste, there was no denying it. The room was as cool and smooth as he was, with a massive antique desk that added just the right amount of classy yet rough-hewn ruggedness, it had the same tough, matter-of-fact edge that its owner possessed in abundance. There were no tacky Christmas decorations in here either, and not a single empty glass from the party – even though Mr L. did have a well-stocked drinks cabinet for entertaining his VIP visitors. This suite needed even less cleaning than the rest of the floor, but that didn't stop Nattie expending far more time and energy in it than she had in any other office.

When she'd finally dusted and polished the main area to perfection, she turned her attention to the adjacent 'executive' washroom; one of Mr Lawson's hard-earned perks. It was here that she'd had her 'particular instance', she recalled fondly. As she began scrubbing the sink with cream cleaner, she permitted herself a little memory.

She'd come in very quietly that morning – still half-asleep, to be honest – and just assumed that it was the security man who'd opened up and switched on the lights. It was only when she'd padded almost all the way across the office and heard the sound of running water from the washroom, that she'd realised it was Mr Lawson who'd beaten her into work yet again.

He'd been standing in front of the wash-basin, unconsciously posing like a pin-up in just the skimpiest of black, thong-like underpants. He'd been splashing water over his chest and under his arms, and as his flight bag had been open beside him, he'd probably just got in from the airport.

Nattie had crept away then, and started on somebody else's office, but the image of that long, bronzed body – clad only in the sauciest of undies – had haunted her brain ever since.

She'd thought of him during lectures, on buses and while buying her modest amounts of shopping. She'd filled every idle minute with that picture of him, made it the focus of her frequent masturbation sessions; even – to her great shame – used the sight of it to concentrate her pleasure while Andy had been making his rather abbreviated and unthrilling love to her.

Was that why they'd split? Andy hadn't been the most perceptive of men, but she wondered if on some subliminal level he'd become aware of his rival in her mind. Maybe so . . . But that was still no excuse for him dumping her just before Christmas. She was willing to bet that Mr Lawson wouldn't have been such a rat to whatever lucky woman *he* was involved with. Putting down the lid of the lavatory, Nattie sat down, stuck out her legs and leaned back. It was Christmas after all, so she decided to give herself a present: a beautiful Mr Lawson fantasy.

Slowly opening her mind, she coaxed the man in question inside. She saw the brown limbs, the tight, muscular bottom, the bulge in those teasing black briefs . . . but the quality of image wasn't clear. The light in the bathroom was too harsh and intrusive, bouncing off the tiles and hurting her eyes. With a sigh, she got up, flipped the switch, and settled down again in the darkness.

In her fantasy, it was slushy romance that initially held sway. They were in a restaurant, dining intimately, with champagne, roses, significant looks, the full bit. Mr Lawson was all smiles, sweet words and compliments . . . Presently, he was escorting her to his limousine and helping her inside it – but with lots of little fondles in the process. Sly gliding strokes tantalised her breasts and bottom; gropes, to put it bluntly . . . In her dream, Nattie's expensive designer frock was so exquisitely sheer and thin that his fingers burned warm where they touched.

In real life, she knew very well that Mr Lawson was a sophisticated and discerning man with impeccable manners; but in fantasyland it was perfectly okay that he behave like an adolescent sex fiend and feel her up at every available opportunity. Within seconds of the car moving off, he was peeling down the top of her cocktail dress and baring her soft warm breasts.

Cocktail dress? Nattie asked of her dreaming self, knowing she'd never actually worn one and probably wouldn't ever want to. In the same way that she'd never ever bother to put up her soft blonde locks in such an elaborate and soignée hairstyle.

But it didn't matter how well-groomed she looked, Mr L. seemed intent on changing all that. Within seconds her hair was down and he'd uncovered her breasts and nipples. Her dark pink nipples that were already as hard as cherry pips. She could easily imagine how his cultured fingertips might feel on her skin, but to make the experience more valid, she unbuttoned her overall, pushed her T-shirt up to her armpits, then cupped her bra-less breasts in her hands. Squeezing herself tightly, she caressed her stoney nipples with her fingers, just as an experienced lover like Mr L. might do. Or Jared, as she liked to think of him at moments like these.

As she stroked and aroused her own breasts, her mind showed Jared overtaking her; moving further . . . He was sliding up her skirt now, running it smoothly over her silky stockings and her even silkier legs. The action was so suave and accomplished that the thought of it, plus her own tender touches at her nipples, made the heart of her sex moisten freely. Jared's phantom fingers slid with sure, practised ease into her frilly, figured satin panties, then delicately stirred her hot flesh.

Wriggling on her impromptu throne, Nattie

longed to recreate *everything* with accuracy: to smoothly unclothe her own sex, then caress it elegantly to pleasure with her fingers. But her tight denim jeans made things awkward, and meant she'd never match the sleek grace of Jared.

Nevertheless, she tried. Skimming down the zip, she opened up her frayed but serviceable denims, inveigled her fingers inside them, and then into her just-as-tatty knickers.

Just as she was about to dive deeper and seek out her clitoris, a noise in the outer office stopped her dead. Desire itself didn't die, but for thirty long seconds her limbs and her body were frozen. There was somebody moving about out there. At the any moment she'd be discovered skulking in her hideout, possibly in the act of masturbation!

As she sat on the toilet, immobile and with her fingers still trapped inside her clothes, she had a flash of quite startling lucidity. The steps outside were uneven and hesitant – not a bit like Mr Lawson's usual confident strides. Yet she still knew it was him. She also got the definite impression he was drunk. As if to confirm her suspicions she heard an angry, muttering voice, then a stumble and a colourful curse.

What the hell was going on? She could imagine anybody getting slightly tiddly on Christmas Eve, even a smooth operator like Mr Lawson. But falling down drunk? Solitary Christmases were for romantic lovers like Natalia Romaine, not for debonair ladykillers like Jared Michael Lawson. Especially as there was a silver-framed photograph of a woman in a prominent position on his desk – an object that Nattie had always studiously ignored.

Even as she thought of the frame, there was a crash, a splintering, and the word 'bitch' perfectly enunciated in his deep-dark, bitter-chocolate voice. 'Bitch,' he growled again as Nattie finally pulled her hand from her jeans and tugged her T-shirt back down to her waist.

'Dammed fucking bitch,' he elaborated with a good deal more violence.

Nattie was behind the bathroom door now, and observing him through a convenient crack between door and jamb. As he swore, she flinched, but then calmed again. He obviously hadn't the slightest awareness of her presence, because he was sitting in his huge, leather covered chair, his long legs stretched and spread, and his straight body tellingly slumped. The silver-framed picture was lying on the floor some feet away, and on the desk before him was a tumbler full of amber fluid that Nattie assumed to be whisky. 'Bitch,' he reiterated, his anger, sorrow, disappointment or whatever seeming to combine with the liquor in erasing his extensive vocabulary.

'Don't need you, you know,' he muttered on, pulling at the buttoms of his shirt. His jacket was already on the floor not far from the picture. 'I can make my own fun . . .' He giggled then – the sound strangely sexy and boyish – and started struggling with his elegant, crocodile-skin belt and the zip of his dove grey trousers.

Holy Christ! though Nattie wildly, recognising immediately what her idol was up to. The very same act that she'd been about to perform.

Beneath the grey designer tailoring were plain dark briefs, but Nattie didn't get much time to study them. Almost immediately his equipment was on view. His penis; so superbly stiff and furiously red with its swollen and shiny-slick glans. She sighed, then wished she hadn't, terrified that the man outside might be sober in an instant if he heard her.

7

Oh God, Mr Lawson, you're beautiful! she thought breathlessly when the immediate danger was past. He was entirely absorbed in his own self-pleasure now; his eyes were closed, his breathing was heavy and he seemed oblivious to everything else in the world but the long bar of flesh in his fingers.

Nattie felt her own sex ache as her fantasy made careful love to his. The woman who'd ditched him or whatever must be mad! she thought, gaining a comforting new perspective on her own recent letdown. If she'd lost a man like Mr Lawson at Christmas, she really would be unhappy. Instead of feeling just mildly upset over an insensitive twerp like Andy.

What's more – she told herself philosophically – if she'd been out celebrating with Andy tonight, she wouldn't have had chance to see this!

Mr Lawson was in motion now, writhing in his deep, executive chair, his lean body bucking, his tanned hands a masturbating blur. He was groaning too; not flinging insults to his silver-framed betrayer anymore, but simply encouraging his own randy efforts with an evocative catalogue of grunts, sighs and broken, unintelligible words.

Andy would have come ages ago, observed Nattie, almost dispassionately. Her ex had a problem with pre-emptive spurting, whereas Mr L. seemed to be going on forever! His erection was invulnerable to his own ferocious fingers. He was wrenching at his flesh like a sex-crazed maniac, his chest awash with sweat and his angry red shaft all coated with the silver of his juices.

Is it the booze? Nattie wondered. Was he so aroused, so hard and so pissed that ejaculation and orgasm were impossible? It certainly seemed so. But

8

if that meant she could watch him for longer, there was no way she was about to complain!

'Oh God,' he moaned, more delectable than ever in his torments. His heels were dragging on the carpet, and he was tossing his head from side to side, dishevelling his usually-neat curls. 'Oh God,' he gasped again, licking his lips, his whole lean face stretched taut in an agony of pleasure. 'Oh, please! I can't —' he babbled, then suddenly his lust-darkened eyes snapped open and his grimace seemed to soften to a smile.

Nattie saw him settle back down into his seat, his cock still rampant, but his body a little more relaxed. It was as if he'd found an agreeable solution to his problem and was gathering his wits for his final implementation.

'Okay . . . Come out. You're going to have to help me with this.' He was looking straight down at his penis, and jiggling it playfully, but his voice was pitched towards the doorway.

If anyone had asked her, Nattie would've sworn that her heart stopped beating then. But nobody was asking her anything, and a moment later Mr Lawson repeated his order, his voice ragged and uneven as he started panting and gasping again.

'Come out. I know you're in there.'

He'd find her eventually, she realised, so there seemed no point in lingering. She pulled up the zip of her jeans and stepped out of the bathroom and the shadows.

'Now how did I know it was going to be you?' he asked, his lazy smile widening and his fingers still toying with his cock. 'You're the girl who always watches me, aren't you? The shy girl . . . The pretty one who never says a word.'

Even though she could move, Nattie couldn't

speak. Dumbstruck she walked towards him, her eyes locked tightly on that rosy pole of manflesh and the narrow brown hand that gripped it.

It was a time for neither debate or explanation. Nattie remained rapt and silent. Mr Lawson said simply, 'Please. Will you help me?'

Driven purely by instinct, she started pulling off her shabby working clothes. This god needed a woman's body around him for his pleasure. And though she recognised her many shortcomings, when it came to the moment she was a female with the necessary anatomy . . .

When her T-shirt came off, he smiled in approval. When she stumbled, struggling out of her close-fitting jeans, he laughed softly – though his brown eyes were benign, not mocking. When she was nude, he reached out towards her, his expression full of raw, burning hunger and his prick pointing straight towards her pussy.

A few moments ago, she'd been bemoaning her own lack of grace, but as Mr Lawson took her hand and helped her to straddle his lap, Nattie found a new and hitherto unknown source of poise. Astonished by her own lithe confidence, and the smooth way her limbs meshed with his, she moved over him, tucked his cock into her body and slid down on it slowly and sensually.

They both sighed as he bucked upwards to fill her completely. He, because she was so obviously the comfort he sought; she, because she'd never been so stretched and so pleasured. Mr Lawson felt vast inside her: his penis so alive, and so hot. His hands closed tightly on her buttocks; first to hold her and soothe her, then to move and guide her in pursuit of the optimum sensation. Her sensation as well as his . . . Without thinking, she leaned forward and braced herself, one hand on his muscular shoulder. The other hand slid quite naturally down to her sex, a fingertip settling delicately on her clitoris to compliment the fullness in her pussy.

'Yes!' mouthed Mr Lawson, the heat in his eyes telling Nattie that he liked what she'd done.

Strangers, yet bonded, they rocked and writhed and swayed together in the cradle of the big leather chair. Nattie had never consciously employed sexual skills before, but now she discovered that she possessed some. Clamping her internal muscles around him, she caressed Mr Lawson with her body and almost shouted with triumph when he whimpered and struggled in response. His large cock seemed to swell up inside her, reaching inwards and bringing pure, bubbling joy to every deep-seated crevice and niche. In a frenzy, she rubbed and pummelled at her clitoris to the rhythm of his pleasure-crazed lunges. For what felt like hours they cried and squirmed and sweated together. Their bodies were mated as if they'd been loving each other for decades, and intended to go on for decades more . . .

But at length the sweet moment came. Nattie's orgasm seemed to fall from the sky like a star, dropping downwards in a glorious incandescent blaze and melding with Mr Lawson's rising surge of release. He cried out hoarsely, then silenced his own mouth with hers, pressing their lips together in a long wet kiss that sealed and perfected their climax.

'I imagine you'll be expected at a party or something now, won't you?' he asked quietly, a good while later. The force of their pleasure seemed to have burnt off the effects of the alcohol somehow, and his voice sounded normal and controlled.

Nattie was lying in his arms now, draped across

his knee, her naked body moist with his semen. Still overwhelmed, she shook her head – unwilling to open her mouth, re-establish hard reality, and highlight the disparity of their lives.

When he spoke, his soft, rich tones were tentative. It seemed unthinkable, and incredible, but to Nattie it almost sounded as if he were pleading.

'I don't suppose you'd consider coming home with me for a fireside feast, would you?' he asked.

'Champagne, nuts, cheese, mince pies: you know the sort of thing . . .' As she sat up straight, to look at him, she caught the tail-end of a glance towards the fallen photo-frame.

'Okay, I admit it . . .' he said, sounding momentarily bitter. 'It was originally planned for somebody else . . .' He paused for a second, as if shaking off a demon, then gave Nattie a warm, open smile, 'But right now, I'd much rather share it with you.'

It was totally crazy, but the decision was effortless. 'I'd love to,' she whispered, then daringly pressed a kiss to his cheek.

Her acceptance seemed to galvanise him. Matching her kiss with one of his own, he urged her up on to her feet, stroking the curve of her hip as he did so. His eyes went dark, then bright with a fresh, new burst of desire; but he grinned in an attempt to contain it. The word 'later' hung delightfully in the air between them, and he pushed his slightly-rising penis back into his briefs, zipped his trousers, then stood up beside her.

'Get your clothes on, pretty girl, and I'll rustle up a taxi.'

Wondering where her knickers were, Nattie watched him run his fingers through this crisp dark hair, then efficiently put the rest of his clothing to rights – no mean feat after she'd rubbed her

12

seeping, sweating body all over him.

As he reached for the telephone, he hesitated. 'Just one more thing,' he said thoughtfully, and Nattie bit her lip, wondering if he'd just changed his mind.

'Merry Christmas, Nattie,' he whispered in her ear as he pulled her still only half-covered body back against him.

So you *do* know my name! she thought happily, pushing her breasts against the cotton of his shirt and realising – all over again – that it was the magical night before Christmas. In spite of his casual mention of nuts and mince pies and stuff, what'd happened in the big leather chair had made her forget the festivity of the season.

But now, held tight in such strong, gorgeous arms, she did remember – and her feeling of goodwill to all men could've lit up every street in the city. 'Merry Christmas, Mr Lawson,' she murmured as she pressed her bare belly against his groin.

Well, at least she knew what to give him as a present!

The Fruits of Learning

I NEVER REALISED I could be this happy, thought Madeleine blissfully as she accepted a peach from Delrina's golden bowl. Laying aside her book, she bit into the fruit's velvet skin, and as its ripe, sweet taste exploded on her tongue she sighed with pleasure, and felt the peach-juice dribble over her chin and drip down on to the slope of her breast. Licking her lips, and taking another large bite, she lolled back amongst the silk-covered cushions, closed her eyes, and remembered how she'd come to this place . . .

It'd all begun when her father couldn't pay the Prince's tribute.

The shame had been terrible, but there'd been worse to come when the Royal Chamberlain had suggested a solution. Madeleine hadn't known which to fear the most: year after year of debt and dishonour as her family struggled to find the money, or the total surrender of her body when she entered the Prince's service.

Madeleine had heard tales of such delicate arrangements, but had always dismissed them as hearsay. The ageing Prince was noted for his over-developed sexual appetites – especially where younger women were concerned – but it seemed preposterous that he could have her by command. Didn't he keep his Byzantine houris for such loathsome purposes? There were three pampered, licentious women, often glimpsed frolicking in the verdant palace gardens, their voluptuous, satin-skinned bodies lightly clad in tiny scraps of cloth of gold. Surely such beauty as theirs was enough to satisfy his Highness's needs? What could he want with a skinny, bookish virgin?

Still, the sacrifice had to be made – it was the only way to avoid Papa's ruin.

Though innocent in body, Madeleine well knew what passed between men and women. An intelligent girl, as well as pretty in her own fragile way, she'd deduced a great deal from her studies of literature and biology. To reproduce, it seemed, a man and woman must couple, and in this joining lay the ultimate pleasure. The touch of a man was supposed to be all that a women might crave, but for her own part, Madeleine was doubtful. She found the notion of a naked man fondling her and mounting her repellent. She knew that in this respect she wasn't like most girls of her age, but she couldn't see any way to change what she felt.

Nevertheless, despite her terrors, Madeleine was aware of her duty. When the day of her summons to the palace came, she followed the Royal Chamberlain without protest and tried stoically not to dwell on her fate.

At the gate of the sumptuous women's quarters, she was met by the Prince's three beauties.

'Don't be afraid, little one,' said Delrina, the tallest and most lovely, giving Madeleine a smile of great

15

sweetness and understanding. 'You'll be safe here with us. And you'll find a new way to be happy.'

Madeleine would have liked to dispute this, but Delrina's gentle charm *was* soothing. The Byzantine woman had eyes that were warm as brown velvet, and her mouth was soft and rosy. Her long, glistening black hair was crowned by a pretty, gilded cap, and like her companions, Nadia and Laurelina, she was sublimely curvaceous, and graced with proudest and lushest of bosoms, a tiny, tiny waist, and hips that flared elegantly yet ripely beneath the frill of her pleated silk skirt – the only garment that covered her body.

Nadia and Laurelina – blonde and redheaded respectively – were both equally enchanting and both wore the same bizarre outfits. They seemed bright-eyed and happy, and not the slightest bit troubled by their captivity. When she looked at them, Madeleine felt confused. She should have despised them for their willing submission, yet all three women had a strange and seductive effect on her, and their presence made her feel quite relaxed. She was still nervous of what the future might hold for her, but her new companions made the fear a little less.

'Come, we'll show you our sanctuary,' said Nadia gently, her green eyes glinting. She took Madeleine's arm and, as they walked, the tip of the concubine's uncovered breast brushed lightly against Madeleine's elbow. The tiny, bouncing contact produced a frisson of intense sensation, and Madeleine felt her whole body turn quivery and glowing. The relaxation she'd felt increased to a strange, heavy lethargy, and her own breasts seemed to swell and start aching. Her simple, woollen gown seemed suddenly too tight and in her belly there was a long, low stirring.

Shaken, she allowed the three young women to lead her down an exquisitely decorated corridor and into a room of yet more opulence and refinement. Elaborately embroidered hangings covered all four walls – except where there were a series of tall, well-filled bookcases and leaded windows trimmed with multicoloured glass – and underfoot there was a thick Persian carpet. The centre of chamber was furnished not with the usual wooden chairs and tables, but with a number of deep, upholstered divans, strewn with cushions and long, satin throws. Through two open arched doorways beyond, Madeleine could see other areas of equal luxury: an inner garden with a marble-lined pool and playing fountain, and a huge, airy, blue and gold tiled bathing room. The air in the chamber was fresh, and circulated freely, yet carried the perfume of roses and musk.

'This is our haven,' murmured Laurelina, gesturing towards the centre of the room with a toss of her burnished red hair.

'Our sanctuary,' whispered Nadia, pressing her breast more closely against Madeleine's arm.

'Our school of love,' finished Delrina with a slow sensuous smile, taking her place at Madeleine's other elbow, as between them, she and Nadia led their charge towards the bathing room. 'This is where we were taught the arts of love by the women who came before us, and they in turn were taught by the those who preceded them.' Reaching out, she touched Madeleine's blushing cheek and let her hand trail slowly downwards, 'This is where you too will learn many skills and accomplishments . . . but not necessarily for the pleasure of the Prince.'

Not sure what the other woman meant, Madeleine allowed herself to be led into the bath-house.

Aren't they his servants? she wondered. His mistresses? How is it that they all seemed so powerful?

As the women undressed her, Madeleine began to shake more and more. First her dress, then her undergarments were peeled away from her pale, waif-like body; as each item of clothing was discarded, all three of the women examined the lightly freckled skin that was revealed. Madeleine's cheeks turned from blush pink to deepest, ruddy crimson as the secrets of her flesh were explored.

She moaned as Delrina took hold of her breasts, one in each soft-skinned hand, and seemed to weigh them and assess their tender firmness. She whimpered and swayed on her feet as Nadia's nimble fingertips slid into her furrow and travelled over each fold and indentation. She cried out hoarsely, and almost fell, as Laurelina drew a single hot fingertip between the cheeks of her bottom, then pushed wickedly at the most-forbidden entrance.

'Please,' begged Madeleine, with no real idea what she asked for as the the three women continued to probe her. Their slender fingers traversed and rubbed until her poor body was melting with excitement. She felt embarrassment and shame, but within and beyond it she felt the dawning of an amazing new knowledge.

For what seemed like an age she was pinned at the centre of a triangle of beauty, her naked female shape its prime focus. Then, as first Delrina, then Nadia and Laurelina withdrew, she cried out at the loss of their touch.

'Come, we will bathe you now,' said Delrina, taking Madeleine's hand in her own, then leading her towards the scented pool.

Used to the spartan facilities of her family's ordinary home, Madeleine was stunned by the richness around her. The slowly lapping water was deep enough at one end to stand in, although the women chose the shallower area in which to carry out their intimate ablutions. Flinging off their skimpy clothing, they joined her in the pool, and set about their task with a gentle enthusiasm. Stirred as she was by the way they'd caressed her, Madeleine accepted everything in a pliant, dreamy silence.

Once again their fingers searched her naked body this time coating it with a dense, creamy lather that slithered like an unguent across her skin. The thick white foam was scented with almonds, and every place it touched seemed to tingle. Madeleine sensed that this too was part of the preparation for pleasure; that within the soap itself there was some esoteric ingredient that aroused her to a heightened sensitivity. She felt herself leaning heavily into every stroke of the washcloth, constantly wishing it would go further and further. Her wet thighs slid apart with little conscious effort, and she sighed when the cloth went between them.

She knew now that a crisis of some kind was approaching, an unknown pinnacle of physical sensation. Every part of her was filled with a deep, sweet yearning, laden with a hunger that she couldn't quite define. Maybe this was the 'desire' the books spoke of: the rapture, the very transports of passion? It seemed almost incomprehensible that she should feel it with these women when the idea of a man made her shudder, and yet somehow she was helpless to resist.

'Surrender, my darling,' murmured Delrina, sliding the washcloth back and forth with great

purpose. 'There's nothing to fear from your body.'
As the dark woman pressed harder, the others also
moved in close: each attending to a different part of
Madeleine, and touching her where they'd touched
her before.

Suddenly, a feeling like no other seemed to burst
between Madeleine's twisting thighs. Heat, light-
ness, and a great and euphoric rush of pleasure. She
could feel the very quick of her womanhood
throbbing, yet the awareness of it seemed to speed
through every bit of her, from her top of her head to
the tips of her toes.

'Yes! Yes!' chanted Nadia and Laurelina in a
chorus as Madeleine collapsed in their arms. She
could no longer support the weight of her body and
would have sunk beneath the water without them.

'That's the first lesson,' she heard Delrina
whisper, then heard no more as the second one
began.

By nightfall, Madeleine had caught up with the
learning of a lifetime. Her three new friends had
brought her time and time to that indescribable
peak, and on each occasion the means had been
different.

Lying naked on her divan, with her skin polished
and gleaming, Madeleine tried to separate each
instance of 'the moment' – but her pleasure-drugged
mind wouldn't work. She seemed only to recall one,
long lambent sequence of bodily enjoyment and sly
caresses in all her secret places. When it was over,
they'd dried her tenderly with a soft linen sheet,
glazed her skin with a blend of sweet oils, then fed
her a meal of fresh fruit and mild cheese, all washed
down with a heady, spiced wine. After only a few
mouthfuls, she'd been sleepy.

Alone now, with Delrina, Nadia and Laurelina retired to a large, shared divan of their own, Madeleine found herself suddenly wakeful and thinking.

Would the Prince expect such liberties from her? Or would he simply require possession of her hymen? She trembled, imagining his gnarled old fingers and his lined and wrinkled mouth doing the things that her companions had done to her. Would she not cringe with distaste if he sucked on her breast, or thrust a bony digit roughly inside her? Would she not die a thousand, shameful deaths if he caressed the velvet cheeks of her bottom, then probed her tiny portal with his tongue? And what if he asked the same of her? Oh, no, it was too horrible to contemplate.

Yet her companions must do such things for him, and they seemed delighted with their lot. They didn't lie awake and worry – although as Madeleine had *that* thought, she realised they weren't sleeping.

On the large divan, a few feet from her own, there were the beginnings of motion in the shadows. Three sets of smooth, naked limbs were combining, and three voices were sighing and gasping. With a sense of fascination, Madeleine realised that her companions were pleasuring themselves: both individually, and presently, in ensemble. Forgetting her worries, and forgetting sleep also, she let her fingers find the cleft of her sex.

The next day passed strangely contentedly, although not in the manner she'd expected.

After being left to bathe alone, and fed again on a delicious light meal, Madeleine was surprised when the women didn't touch her. She'd anticipated further lessons and further touching, and been perplexed when none were forthcoming. Instead, Delrina had led her to the bookcases, and encouraged her to choose the choicest volumes.

'All these books contain knowledge that will help you with your duties. You must read, so you'll know what we know.'

Loving books as she did, Madeleine had soon forgotten her disappointment. The private library was a wondrous hoard of knowledge, and as arousing in its way as the long, shared hours of yesterday. Each book was a classic of pornography. As she read – and read and read and read – Madeleine soon grew both learned and fevered. Every picture seemed to remind her of the touch of Delrina's lips, or the way Laurelina's fingertips could seek out, and find, the most discreet and receptive of pleasure-nodes, then tantalise them to the very edge of madness. Every line or paragraph of uncensored prose seemed to conjure up the taste of Nadia's sweat.

When evening came, Madeleine could recall little of the day. Her mind was a blur of sensual images, and her slender body a furnace of desire. A great well of heat that didn't even cool when finally the dreaded summons arrived.

This time, their bathing was even more scrupulous than yesterday, but in the water there were only acts of cleansing. In a daze, though feeling far less fearful than she'd expected, Madeleine let the other three adorn her. Washed and creamed with oils and lotions, she lay back and let Delrina trim her fluff of pubic curls, then daub her folds with a gentle, perfumed rouge. She allowed her nipples to be coloured too, then be painted with more oil so they'd shine. The last refinement was a diamond in her navel.

When her face too had been delicately painted, she let the women dress her in the same golden garments that they wore, and brush her brown hair to a glossy, rippling fall.

'The Lady Madeleine, my Lord,' announced Delrina at the door of the Prince's chamber.

Bowing low, Madeleine stepped forward, feeling more defiance – and desire – than fear now. Yes, she'd give herself to this ancient, lusty sovereign; but she'd use *him* to satisfy *her* rising appetites just as he'd be using her to slake his own.

'I am yours, my Lord,' she said boldly, speaking the words just as she been instructed. Then, with all the grace she could muster, she lay back on the silk divan before him and bared her treasure to his old, but piercing eyes.

Not daring to look at his face now the moment of surrender had arrived, Madeleine shivered as she heard the sibilant rustle of his heavy, brocade-trimmed robes.

'How lovely you are, my young one,' he murmured. 'How precious and how deliciously ripe.' His quavering voice had a soft, kindly ring to it – and as she absorbed this, her revulsion seemed to lessen. Perhaps there would be *real* joy here after all?

'Let us begin,' he said quietly, when what felt like an age of time had passed.

Eyes tightly shut, Madeleine heard more rustling, then felt the heat of a body close to hers. Gentle hands parted her thighs, and shuddering wildly she tried to relax.

Open . . . More and more open . . . She could almost feel an alien flesh touch hers . . . Bracing herself for the Prince's rigid penis, she cried out when the kiss of contact came.

Crying again, and feeling something quite different to what she'd been expecting, Madeleine let her closed eyes open, and got the most beautiful and unexpected of surprises.

She saw power and eroticism in the Prince's aged face, and the light of simple pleasure there too. The surprise was that he was seated on his throne still, with his stately robes thrown negligently open and his penis clasped tightly in his fist.

When as his old eyes fluttered closed in rapture, Madeleine felt her own flesh leap and judder. Smiling, laughing, almost crying, she looked down towards the apex of her thighs . . . and saw Delrina with her red mouth hard at work.

Still smiling now, Madeleine took another greedy bite of her peach.

'I only want to *see* your beauty, gentle Madeleine,' the Prince had said later, 'and to see you learn the joys of pleasure from my darlings.'

The old man she'd so feared didn't want to touch her at all, she now realised. All he wanted was to watch as his women made love to her. A simple privilege she was happy to permit him. Plying her with wine afterwards, and looking fondly on her flushed and sweating body, he'd said that she need only stay at the palace for a little while longer, then she was free to leave, with her father's debts paid.

But do I want to leave? Madeleine pondered, chewing her mouthful of succulent peach-flesh and starting to wriggle against the satin of her cushions. Now that all's well, and I understand what the Prince *really* needs, it might be nice to stay here and enjoy his wondrous library; to fully savour the delicious fruits of learning.

Madeleine smiled happily as she considered this,

but before she could reach for her book, or even take another bite of peach, both the book and the fruit were quite forgotten.

Closing her eyes, she arched languorously on her bed of silken comfort, and as the peach slipped and fell from her fingers, a darting tongue lapped her breast clean of its juice . . .

A Thing of Beauty

IT WAS THE most beautiful thing I'd ever seen, but all it made me do was want to cry. I ran my fingers slowly over the lace, the boning, and the tiny appliqué flowers, and wondered what on earth had possessed me to buy something so ridiculous, so expensive and so useless. It was too late now, the time for sexy lingerie was long past. Not even a pure silk, gunmetal blue basque could salvage the ruins of my marriage.

I'd sent for it on impulse, from a flyer that'd fallen out of a magazine. It was one of those 'today's woman' glossies that I'd bought for an article on 'Putting the Spice Back into your Relationship'. I was clutching at straws really – doubly so in the case of the basque – because I don't think I've ever finished one of those oh-so-helpful articles. They all seemed so unreal and pretentious, as if they were written for tall blonde superwomen who wouldn't have problems in the first place, and probably wore slinky undies anyway.

Even so, I'd sent for the basque, strangely inspired because it looked so pretty, and because the model wasn't blonde, and even looked a little bit like me. She was more eye-catchingly glamorous, of course, but the raw material was the same. Straight nut-brown hair, medium figure, blue eyes. I was quite good-looking in my own way too.

Not that Mike had noticed lately . . .

Oh, he'd never been cruel or unkind to me, and I don't think he had the time to have an affair – he was too busy and preoccupied with his work. It was just that he'd stopped really looking at me, stopped meaning it when he kissed me goodbye every morning, stopped having either the interest or the energy for anything more than the most perfunctory and uninspiring lovemaking.

It hadn't always been like that. We'd been desperate for each other when we'd first fallen in love. I'd bought pretty undies then too. I remembered the gorgeous white lace bra and knickers I'd worn under my wedding dress – and the frenzied fervent way that Mike had stripped them off me. Then he made love to me, murmuring 'Jenny, oh, Jenny, I love you' as our pleasure rose up and overwhelmed us.

Somehow, though, apathy had crept in. I couldn't quite remember when the wildness had gone out of what happened between us in bed; when Mike had stopped reaching for me so often; when his being self-employed had started meaning self-absorbed; when I'd started reading voraciously, taking evening courses, and buying five packs of Marks & Spencers knickers instead of sheer satin and frills.

The blame was shared, I knew. Mike had lost sight of his home life in his desire to develop his business. But it was me who'd felt resentful, sought distraction, and hadn't tried to understand. When I'd wanted romance, I'd turned to my imagination instead of to the man I loved. The daydreams had turned into hastily scribbled-down stories that I'd polish up at my creative writing class. We'd both of us turned in on ourselves, instead of reaching out to each other.

It was only when I realised that my so-called love stories were always pretty lacklustre that it dawned on me how truly drab my own love story was. I'd been looking for a picture of an ideal hero, but I'd found no-one amongst the sleekly groomed male models in my magazine. I wanted him to be sandy-haired, handsome but not clichéd, quite beautiful but in a rugged sort of way. He had to be tall, and wear glasses, and – I realised suddenly – look exactly the way Mike had looked, in the early happy days of our marriage.

The revelation left me shaking, befuddled, confused. Which might account for me thinking that the purchase of a single set of overpriced lingerie could solve matters. The flyer had fallen out of the very same magazine I'd been seeking my dream man in. But when the basque had arrived, so had the tears. For a while I sobbed furiously at my own futility and silliness, then decided to make the best of things. I'd get my money's worth out of all that extravagant satin!

In the old days, Friday had always been our best night – the night when the pure physical fireworks had gone off and our lovemaking had always hit its highs. Armed with gladrags, I tried to recreate the same conditions. I went mad on a special dinner, bought a wine we both liked; even took an afternoon off work to preen and pamper myself. I blow-dried my hair, waxed some bits of me and rubbed perfumed body cream into others. I did a special, but subtle make-up that ought to withstand the rigours of being ardently made love to. I made myself as beautiful as I could, then I put on my basque and its matching panties, some sheer, finely-seamed stockings, my best robe, and waited . . .

And waited and waited and waited.

At first the anticipation was lovely. It was so exciting to be building myself up to such heights again – waiting for my handsome husband with desire and sex on my mind. Sipping a glass of wine, I found myself filled with arousal for the first time in ages, my body tingling in its elegant silk and lace casing, longing for the moment when Mike's strong hands would release me from its sensuous confines. I began to re-live some of the memorable moments of our former lovemaking: the times we'd clung to each other, sobbing with pleasure, vowing to love one another always, and always with the same sweet passion.

I remembered one Friday when Mike had kissed every inch of my body, making me whimper with longing before finally ravishing me. He'd always been a good lover, always thoughtful, watching out for my satisfaction almost above his own. At least that was how it'd been in the beginning, before we'd begun to retreat to opposite corners of the universe. I stroked the cool, steely-coloured satin that shaped me, and made a conscious vow. Tonight, we'd pull ourselves back together again. If I wanted it hard enough I could get it. I breathed in, fluffed my hair, and checked my seams. I *could* make Mike start looking again!

Another hour, and another glass of wine later, I was feeling less optimistic. I was also feeling foolish, staring glumly at myself in the mirror, dressed up as a high-class tart for a man who probably wasn't interested. My suspenders looked stupid. My pushed-up bosom gross. My panties were too see-through, too sleazy, too little and yet far too much.

By ten, it was obvious he wasn't coming home, and just as the tears began, I got the call. 'A business meeting.' 'Don't worry.' I'll get a Chinese.' 'Don't wait up.'

It was only what often happened, but this time, done up in my beautiful things, it hurt a hundred times harder. 'I said, 'Yes.' 'It's okay.' 'No worries.' but inside my heart was dying. I put down the phone, scraped the ruined dinner into the waste bin, and drank another glass of wine in one long swallow. I could have finished the whole lot, but I even felt too miserable to get drunk.

In the bedroom, I unhooked, unlaced and unsuspendered myself, then cried again over my beautiful shimmering basque; so perfect, so seductive . . . and so pointless.

Bawling like a baby, in despair, I pushed it roughly in the drawer so I didn't have to look at it. I struggled into a serviceable cotton nightie, brushed my teeth, and crawled into bed, not expecting to sleep, but surprisingly, nodding off after a few cheerless minutes.

I don't know how long it was before the dream began. It could have been moments, or it could have been hours. I only knew that somehow I'd travelled in time, and gone back to those wonderful days – especially those Fridays – when Mike and I had been so close.

I could feel his warm body lying along side mine, his front against my back, like spoons. He felt so strong, and I felt so secure. I snuggled myself to his shape, then smiled with joy in my haziness. The way Mike pressed himself to me let me know that we really were back in those glorious, desire-filled times. He was naked and my nightie had crawled up over my hips; I could feel how he wanted me. How he needed me. And in an instant, I realised how much I'd never stopped wanting him.

Sighing, I tried to turn over, but he held me still, kissing the back of my neck, his lips firm and moist against my ear. His arms came around me, and his hands caressed me, travelling slowly over my finely quivering curves. Their progress was sweet and familiar, yet strangely and poignantly tentative. I felt him asking silently for my permission . . . and my forgiveness. I could swear I felt tears on the side of my neck – and not mine because I was too excited. Turning my face, I kissed the edge of his jaw, then pushed my body backwards against him, granting the permission he craved. With a low groan, he began to explore me, seeking out my warmest most sensitive zones, then finding them with sureness and skill. His fingertips travelled to all my softest chinks and crannies, then dabbled and dipped and stroked, making me whimper and squirm with delight.

Oh, it was so good, so real. So like those wonderful nights in the marvellous first months of our marriage. I *was* crying again now, but with pleasure, as Mike's fingers took me soaring to the peak. Once. Twice. Three times.

While I was still in heaven, he gently rolled me towards him, and on to my back, then moved his long, warm body over me. I was eager and shamelessly wanton, parting my thighs and pushing myself at him – making the way smooth and easy for his manhood.

As he entered me, he kissed me too, taking my lips with a slow, reverent beauty. I cried out and he

31

seemed to drink the sound straight from my mouth, to feed on it in the same way that his lips and his kiss nourished me. The famine of our love was over, and ravenous, we dove into a feast. I sensed Mike trying to hold back, trying to prolong the experience for me, but the need in us both was too great.

After just a few minutes we were shouting, crying, clinging to each other; clutching madly at each other's backs as an implosion of ecstasy engulfed us. Bereft of magic and oneness for so long, we were both swept away by the force of it. I wanted to talk and laugh, to reassure Mike and thank him, pledge that whatever happened in the future, we'd never drift apart again – but within seconds I was sinking fast into sleep. The last thing I remember was tears again. Mine trickling happily down my cheeks, and Mike's against my neck as I held him.

The next morning I awoke still full of happiness. I was filled with questions too, and puzzlement over the irony of timing. Just when I'd thought my last try had failed, it seemed that I needn't have tried anyway. Mike himself had made the first move.

I wanted desperately to ask some of those questions, but instead I let them wait – while we made lazy, wordless, Saturday lie-in love, and our bodies said everything for us.

'Why now?' I asked finally, when Mike brought me coffee in bed, and a rose still dewy from the garden. 'Because I saw this,' he answered sheepishly, picking up something from a drawer he'd just pulled open. 'I saw it poking out, and when I realised what it was, I realised you hadn't given up on me after all . . .'

In his hands he held my pretty blue basque, and

as I watched him, he stroked its delicate, flower-trimmed panels, then held it out shyly towards me.

'Will you wear it?' he asked, his voice rich with a dozen other questions as he waited for me to take it from him.

'Yes, I will,' I murmured, reaching out, 'I'll wear it whenever I think we need it. *Either* of us . . .'

He smiled as our fingers met across the lace, his face bright with love and relief.

Silk and satin aren't the only things of beauty . . .

The Gardener's Boy

ENGLAND IS A STRANGE old place: wonderful, fascinating, but strange. And I think I found the very strangest part of it, that summer when I stayed at Flitwick Hall.

I was running away, really, running as far and fast as I could from heavy emotional troubles. So that beautiful and magical house, far away across the Atlantic in England, seemed like just the kind of hideout I needed.

The invitation to visit the Flitwicks, my English relations, had been around for years. I'd always wanted to visit them, but until that summer I'd never had the chance. When I finally turned up, it was purely a spur of the moment thing, and consequently the house was all but empty. There was only a skeleton staff in residence, to take care of one nutty, reclusive old great-aunt I'd never even known that I had.

My troubles? A man, naturally, and the heartache of love turning bad. Ellery and I had been a hot number for a year, a solid couple so I thought, but one day we'd suddenly started arguing, then realised we weren't a number after all. The parting had been acrimonious, and I'd left with my soul feeling bruised. Two days later I'd also realised I was pregnant – from a meaningless, pleasureless encounter just hours before our final bitter fight.

Now Marylou Deschanel is no coward, I'll tell you, but this time I took the easy way out. I booked straight into a clinic and had an abortion, then went searching for my distant English roots in an effort to diminish the aching void.

Flitwick Hall was the prettiest place you could imagine – a mellow, gilded fairy-house that seemed to glow in the high summer sun. It was still and quiet and tranquil, yet it had a strange air of sexiness about it too; a muted brooding magic that soon set my recovery in motion. Although I've a feeling *that*'d already started when I got there.

Aunt Deebee was a frail old thing, who rarely, if ever, went outside. Even so, she seemed happy enough in her own way: all alone in her cool, shady parlour, smiling fondly at her albums of photos, and reading letters that were yellowing with age. I liked her very much, but all the same I was happy to be left to my own devices. I didn't think Aunt Deebee would understand me . . . because I couldn't really understand myself.

How the devil could I already be feeling horny again, after everything that'd happened with Ellery? I was though . . . Sex seemed to obsess me. I'd started maturbating only days after my surgery, and on the train that'd brought me down from London, I'd caught myself checking out the various travelling males. There'd been one who'd particularly turned me on. He'd been dark, and young, and really, really cute, with long hair and a deeply sweet expression. He'd looked up too, and caught me staring, then smiled the most dazzling, delicious and downright pussy-melting smile that I'd ever seen in my life. I'd been just about to say 'Hi', when the train had pulled into the station, and after everyone had finished hassling about with luggage my sexy-looking dreamboat had gone.

He was a wonderful fantasy though; and as I wandered aimlessly around the gardens at the Hall, his image kept returning to my mind. Especially when I found the little summerhouse . . .

It was a kind of ornamental cabin – what the architecture books called a 'folly' – about a mile from the Hall itself, and hidden away in a thick stand of trees. Sitting pretty in a tiny clearing it was like a gingerbread house straight out of Hans Christian Andersen, and it had a porch and its own enchanted oak tree. I'd never seen a place quite as lovely. As I lay down out in front of it to sun myself, I kept thinking of my dream guy from the train.

I imagined him coming through the trees towards me, emerging next to the oak, then kneeling down on the deck beside me. He'd start touching me and he'd be gentle. His fingers would stroke and smooth and heal. They'd find their own way to all my wounded places, then restore me with the pleasure of good sex.

I had my eyes tightly closed, but with my inner eye I could clearly see him smiling. *His* eyes were brown as autumn leaves and as bright as the brilliant summer sun. As my own hands settled lightly on my body, I could've sworn I saw him wink to urge me on.

As I stroked myself my fingers turned into his, and when they went between my legs, I gave a sigh. I couldn't believe how comfortable it felt. All the guilt about feeling sexy after losing my baby had disappeared, and the hot sensations felt honest and wholesome again. As I quivered, I thanked my secret lover.

'Oh, yes! Oh God, yes!' I gasped, then came with a supernatural quickness. It was a rich, rounded, almost earthy orgasm. I was drowning in a deep well of pleasure with a stranger's handsome face in my mind.

When I'd calmed down, I decided it was time to make tracks back to the Hall. But as I brushed down my skirt and stepped in my shoes, I felt a powerful sensation of being watched, an awareness so strong it gave me gooseflesh. I looked around, but there was no-one in the glade, and no-one hiding out amongst the trees. The whole neighbourhood of the cottage was deserted; so, as I made my way back towards the big house, I decided I'd had a little too much sun. Or too much of something else just as warming.

I didn't mention my spooky feelings to Aunt Deebee, but when we talked a while that night, she looked at me, her blue eyes suddenly sharper. 'Now don't forget to wear a hat in the sun tomorrow, my dear,' she said, her voice kind of vague and dreamy-sounding. 'We don't want you seeing things, do we?'

I told her I was usually okay in hot sun, but next day, I found a battered old sunhat in the cupboard, and put it on before I ventured outdoors. It was a pretty thing with a big round straw brim, but it didn't make the slightest bit of difference . . .

I still saw things.

When I arrived at the summerhouse, there was a sleeping figure lying out in the glade: a young man with shiny dark hair and smooth, bronzed skin. Most of which I could see, because he was naked as the day he'd been born!

I didn't say anything. I hardly dare breathe. He was lying on his front, taking the sun on his broad, gleaming back, and his ass was the finest I'd ever seen. His face was turned towards me, pillowed on his muscular arms, and there was a naughty little smile on his face, as if he knew he was being admired, but wasn't letting on.

The *really* crazy thing was that he looked exactly like my Adonis from the train. Younger, maybe, and rougher somehow, but the resemblance was truly amazing. And I couldn't help but think about his dick.

Would be be big or small? Wide or slender? Circumcised or a natural un-cut? Jesus, my thoughts were outrageous! But I couldn't stop myself . . . All I could do was imagine him turning over, stroking himself lazily – then getting hard. And as I thought *that*, his eyes fluttered open.

'I . . . um . . .' I began nervously, then shut up. Because my nature boy was getting to his feet . . . and he wasn't a boy after all. No way!

Before me stood a big, beautiful, grown-up man with a swaying sex that was long and already half-hard.

'Pardon me, ma'am, but I didn't think there'd be anybody here today.'

His voice was as pretty as his dick. Very polite, very English, but not the kind of English I'd expected. It was a soft, very sonorous voice, kind of rich and countrified, and laced with an echo of the land.

'I just arrived. I'm staying at the big house. I sort of found this place yesterday and thought I might spend some time here,' I babbled, wondering why I was explaining myself to a bare-assed man.

'Beg pardon,' he apologised again, although he

didn't make a move to get dressed. 'I hope I didn't frighten you, ma'am. I'm the gardener's boy, ma'am, and it's my break . . . I was just having a quick forty winks.'

I wasn't quite sure what 'forty winks' was but I couldn't stop staring. He was a god; a hunk; totally drop-dead gorgeous, with the body of an athlete or a boxer, but the face of an angel of love. His cock was the ultimate in pure maleness; standing up like a club now, thick and dark.

'Sorry about that, ma'am,' he murmured, looking down, 'but I don't often meet pretty women in the woods.'

'It's . . . er . . . It's okay,' I mumbled like a dummy, wishing I could say that it was far more than 'okay', and that he could flash a treasure like that at me anytime. 'I'm Marylou Deschanel, from Portland, Maine, and Mrs Flitwick is my aunt, twice removed.'

'Sean Collyer, ma'am,' he answered, nodding his head respectfully – which looked incongruous with a hard-on that size.

I had to admire the guy though; not only for the beauty of his body, but also for his lack of inhibition. Most American men I know would have been blushing beet red and covering themselves up with their shirts. But not my bare-bottomed Brit. He just stood there in all his rampant glory, and I wished to hell I dare reach out and touch.

I'd best be off then, Miss Deschanel,' he said, his voice as unperturbed as his attitude, 'I wouldn't want to disturb you any more.'

Some disturbance, I thought, watching the long easy swing of his dick as he bent gracefully and reached for his clothes. I'd never have thought putting clothes on could be as sexy as stripping them off, but somehow this Sean changed my mind.

Even though his underwear was absolutely the weirdest . . .

First, he pulled on a thick, creamy-coloured vest, sort of woolly, with long sleeves and buttons. Then came his underpants, which were full-length 'combination' affairs in the same chunky fabric, but looked as horny as the skimpiest of jockstraps. Especially with a big erection inside them!

'Look, Sean,' I began, feeling bold enough to use his first name, 'you don't have to go on my account. Please stay . . . We could talk a while.'

My rough, outdoors-man just smiled – the same smile that the guy on the train had smiled, the grin that made me hot – then flicked his braces neatly up over his shoulders and pulled on a dark linen waistcoat. The heat of the day was stifling already, yet his heavy clothes didn't seem to bother him one bit.

'Best not, ma'am,' he said sturdily, and touched his fingers to his forelock just like the farmboys in the stupid old movies. Then, before I could protest, he was leaving, his long, easy stride taking him away so fast that I wondered if I'd just imagined him.

Maybe I *had* imagined him? If I had, I couldn't forget him. Inspired by his example, I peeled off my T-shirt and skirt, and just left on my tiny white panties. As I applied a coat of sunblock, I conjured up those long capable-looking fingers of his, and pretended it was him working the cool, creamy goop across my skin. I knew he'd be able to reach all the awkward places: the middle of my shoulders, the slope of my back, and the round, curvy cheeks of my rear.

Rolling on to my front I imagined him dealing with the easy places too, his fingers palpating the

40

tips of my breasts and filling them with pleasure and heat. I could almost feel those fingertips sliding down me, then slipping lower and toying with the folds of my sex. He'd slide one finger right into me, one manly elegant finger, and twist it till I wailed with delight.

Without thinking, I made thought into deed, using my own hands to act out the fantasy. Pushing my hand into my panties, I stroked my own flesh with intensity. I rubbed harder than a gentle gardener ever would. Fingering with rhythmic swirling's, I brought my body to a fine burning climax, as a pair of brown eyes seemed to watch. Their pupils widened as my body bucked and heaved, then darkened as I groaned in release.

The sensation of being watched was so intense that I soared a second time, when usually it only happened once. My legs waved, and my butt bounced. As I came with a cry, I saw a tiny flicker of movement to my right. It was just a change in the pattern of shadows, or a breeze in the trees, but I prayed it was my handsome gardener's boy.

I didn't venture out until after lunch the next day; and when I did, the heat lay heavy on my back. I could hear bees droning in the long grass, smell the scent of the pollen-filled flowers, and I felt so full of the simple joys of living that when Sean wasn't waiting by the summerhouse it hit me like a cruel, hard shock.

I'd been so sure that he'd be there – either naked or clothed – that his absence hurt me far more than anything Ellery had ever done.

I tried to pull myself together . . .

Yeah, I'd had some fun yesterday, but that was no reason to get uptight. Sean was a worker on the estate, a guy who'd just happened to take his clothes off. He and I weren't a number, any more than Ellery and I. There was no way my handsome Sean had let me down.

Shucking off my vest and skirt, I sat down on the porch and applied some sunblock, still wishing for a pair of male hands to spread it. I'd decided to leave off my panties today, and so when my body was coated I stretched out naked, and surrendered to the mercies of the sun.

For a while I just toasted, letting the golden warmth soak into my bones I forgot my worries and I forgot my disappointment, and I hardly even noticed going to sleep.

I awoke in the coolness of a shadow, and felt my body being oh-so gently fondled. Someone was applying more sunblock for me, slicking it thicking over my thighs and my ass.

Sean! I thought joyfully, but when I rolled over I got one helluva shock. I was alone, the porch was empty, and the extra sunblock only existed in my mind.

I felt giddy for a moment, disorientated and deeply off-balance. It was impossible to believe he wasn't with me, and just when I managed to accept it, I just as quickly realised that he *was*!

The gardener's boy leaning nonchalantly against the side of the oak tree, a slow, sassy smile on his face.

'No drawers today, ma'am?' he enquired and nodded in the direction of my pussy.

'Er . . . no,' I answered, still bemused. So he *had* seen me yesterday after all . . .

'You were watching me – yesterday . . . Weren't you?' I demanded, sitting up, and trying desperately not to grab for my clothes. *He* hadn't been embarrassed naked, so goddammit, neither would I!

42

I was proud of my body, and I liked it – and I wanted *him* to like it just as much!

And he did.

'You're a beautiful woman, Miss Deschanel,' he said, ambling towards me from the deep shade. 'A man'd have to be six feet under not to look at you.'

Just the way he said it set a light in me, and when he dropped down to his knees, then reached out and laid a hand on my breast, it wasn't the hot sun that made my body glow.

Everything seemed to happen naturally, as if I'd been waiting for his fingers all my life. Or at least since long before my 'troubles'. Somehow, it was as if Sean knew exactly what ailed me and touching was his way to make me well. There was no roughness about his hands, none of the hard skin that a manual labourer should have had . . . His caress was as light as thistledown and as cool as a shaded mountain pool. His fingers cruised across me like an unction, a blessed balm against the heat of the day. As he stroked me, his huge brown eyes held mine. They were soul-dark with some ancient, rustic mystery, something primitive I couldn't comprehend. I'd been with some sophisticated men in my time, but this fey country boy with his subtle smiling strength had more charisma than them all put together. Mad to get him, I cried out and strained my body close to his.

'Hush, ma'am,' he whispered against my lips, his fingers sliding slowly into my sex. My softly gorged, slippery, needful sex . . .

With no guidance from me, he found my sweet-spot immediately; the minute patch of skin beneath the head of my clitoris that was so sensitive I could hardly bear it touched.

'Hush, ma'am . . . Rest easy . . . I've got you . . .'

43

he mumured again, as I screamed and went rigid in his arms while a starburst of an orgasm consumed me.

It was impossible how quickly I'd come. And how strongly. He'd done next to nothing and I was in heaven, yet with other men it had often taken hours.

Slumped like a rag-doll against him I tried to recover and to think. I knew nothing about him, but I'd trusted him completely; he'd taken hold of both my body and my heart. My sweat had soaked clean through his undershirt, and my sap was dry already on his hand. I'd behaved madly, badly and riskily, yet I was certain I'd done the right thing.

'Are you all right now, Miss Deschanel?' Sean enquired as I looked up into his eyes. His olde worlde formality was so endearing, it made me want even more of him. I wanted him out of those clumsy woollen trousers; out of those boots; out of those wacky 'drawers' of his. I wanted him as beautiful and naked as he had been yesterday, but with his long, lovely dick deep inside me – as the true, final proof that I was cured.

'I'm great, Sean. I'm fine. But I could be better . . .' I gave him my most come-on look, 'That is, if you kinda get my drift?'

He didn't need asking or telling. With a bewitching, almost edible smile, he started unlacing his stout boots, and in no time at all he was wriggling his way out of his underwear – his sun-browned body primed for action.

Boy, how I wanted him! How I wanted *that*. Leaping up, and reaching for his hand, I nodded towards the door of the cottage. Now the crunch had come, I really *did* feel bashful. I didn't think I could make it in the great outdoors, at least not on our very first time.

44

I hauled at his hand, but Sean wouldn't move. He stood stubbornly on the porch, rooted to the spot, with an expression of real fear on his face.

'What's the matter?' I asked, feeling a little spooked myself. Sean was tough and rugged, genuinely and fundamentally strong, yet suddenly something had fazed him. Something about going 'inside'.

'I can't go in there, Miss Marylou,' he said, his deep voice barely a whisper.

'Why not?' I persisted. The summerhouse was so cosy and so cute.

'Because I can't,' he answered simply, 'I have to stay outside . . . I can't go into any kind of dwelling.'

'But that's n —' I began, only to lose the thread in an instant when Sean picked me up in his arms. Holding me as if I weighed nothing, he carried me across to the big oak tree and set me down on the turf in its shade.

'We'll be safe here, my sweeting,' he said softly, lying down beside me, his hands already moving on my flesh. 'Nothing can harm us out here.'

I forgot my objections. I almost forgot my own name. Sean's lovemaking was so complete, so delicate and so caring, the fact we were outdoors in the open air seemed irrelevant. I felt his fingers in my furrow and his mouth on my breasts, sucking one, and then the other till I moaned.

When I could bear no more, and I was clawing at his body like a mad thing, he gently parted my legs and slid into me, his possession as smooth as in a dream.

Inside me, he felt hard and massive, like the limb of a tree, yet there was no discomfort, no awkwardness and no pain. He moved like a wildcat gliding sleekly through the forest, or a stream flowing unstoppably to the sea. He did not displace or force or exert, but his sex seemed to fit into mine the same way the air we breathed hugged the soil beneath my back.

Our union was timeless, effortless, and ineffable, and when I soared I thought I'd never come down. But as I clung to him, and felt the pleasure start to shake his mighty frame, I was shocked when Sean pulled himself free of me. I protested, clamouring and grabbing at him; then he replaced his rigid cock with two strong fingers and I came again, far harder than before. With his essence pulsing out across my thighs . . .

'Not inside . . .' he gasped, his handsome face ruddy and contorted, 'Oh, no, not ever inside . . .'

It didn't make sense – but neither did getting laid beneath a tree in the sunshine by an Englishman I'd only known a day. With a sleepy sigh, I gave up trying to think about it and just enjoyed his silky semen on my skin.

When I finally woke up again, Sean was gone, but there was a bunch of wild flowers lying in my lap. Their scent was heady and vital, golden and romantic, and I felt more cherished than I had done in years. I missed him but I loved the things he'd done . . .

'I met your gardener's boy today,' I said to Aunt Deebee over dinner. 'He seems like a really nice guy.'

'Who?' my aunt said, her voice all reedy and shocked.

'Sean. The gardener's boy.'

'Oh. Oh, my goodness . . . Has he come back?' Her lined face had a trancelike expression on it, yet in the soft light she looked lovely and quite young.

'Yeah. Has he been somewhere?'

'The last time I saw Sean was when I came here to be married. I was twenty-two. I met him in the woods again and again. But it had to stop, because I really loved Ernest, my fiancé, and being with Sean was very very wrong . . .'

It didn't make a lot of sense then, but afterwards, I kind of got the gist. My handsome young Sean had been killed several centuries ago, shot because a daughter of the house at the time had been crazy enough to smuggle him inside. Her father had gone berserk when he'd found Sean naked in her bedroom. He'd used a blunderbuss to turn him into a ghost!

It seemed *I* was just the latest in a long line of Flitwick women who'd seen 'the gardener's boy', but when pressed for more details of her sighting, Aunt Deebee had turned decidedly coy.

Had all of us *felt* as well as seen him?

The weirdest thing was that I wasn't even scared, just disappointed, because I supposed I'd lost him now. Illusions tend to vanish when you know what they are.

I didn't take my clothes off the next day. There didn't seem an awful lot of point. I just slithered the old cream on my face and arms, then lay down to doze in the sun.

The tremors woke me up very gradually. Cool, probing fingers were sneaking along the inside of my thigh, and heading boldly for the furnace of my sex.

It's a dream, Marylou, I told myself. The sun's too hot. You should've worn the hat again. You're hallucinating.

When the fingertips dove deep into my womanhood, I kept my eyes scrunched resolutely

47

shut. When the pad of a forefinger danced lightly on my clitoris, I still didn't dare take a look. What was happening to me was probably all a fantasy, but if it was one I wanted it to last.

Suddenly, though, I came, and felt my shaking self held tight and sure and safe – against a familiar, solid, man-smelling body that protected me with a tender loving care.

'But you . . . you're . . .' I stammered, as I finally met his big brown eyes.

'Yes, I certainly am, Miss Marylou,' said Seán Collyer – the apparition – very softly. 'But I couldn't let a lady down, could I?'

'No, you certainly couldn't,' I said happily in answer, and started tugging at the buttons on his fly.

Finders Keepers

Dear Jeremy,

*I can't thank you enough for handing in my pendant.
You can't imagine how much it means to me. A money
reward seems sordid somehow, so may I treat you to a
night out instead? I've enclosed details of where and
when we can meet, and I look forward to showing my
appreciation: my PROFOUND appreciation.*

Anna Caspell (Mrs)

When he'd first read the letter, Jem Hathaway had
been disappointed. The pendant he'd handed in
must've cost a fortune and he'd been hoping for a
cash reward. It was a bit of a mystery how a thing so
obviously expensive had turned up outside his
scruffy dump – the house he shared with half a
dozen other guys, all equally as hard up as he was –
but he hadn't asked questions, just dropped it in at
the local police station. He was puzzled too, by the
bobby-on-duty's reaction. The man had grinned
broadly. No, he'd smirked from ear to ear as if
someone had cracked a dirty joke, told Jem there
was a reward, then nudged his mate behind the

counter in the ribs, muttering what sounded like 'jammy young bastard'!

Jem had wondered what the man found so funny, but in a police station he didn't like to ask. He just hoped the reward would be decent, because his meagre giro went nowhere. He'd been out of work for several months now, and jobs were getting scarcer all the time. Even a fiver would make life easier.

A couple of days later the letter had arrived, and it'd seemed that all he was going to get was a night out with an over-fussy, middle-aged widow – a reward that'd be over in a few hours, and probably a pain while it lasted. After a bit of thought, he'd told himself not be such an ungrateful swine, and decided the poor old biddy must be lonely.

But now, when it came to it, money was the last thing on his mind. Staring across the busy hotel foyer, he felt like pinching himself. There was a woman sitting waiting on a velvet-covered chaise-longue, about five yards away from him: the most beautiful woman he'd ever seen. She wore a black, heart-shaped pendant around her long, slender throat, and she was in exactly the right place at exactly the right time. She could only be Anna Caspell (Mrs).

Why didn't I realise? thought Jem, feeling numb: that fancy, flowing handwriting; the sexy pink notepaper; the heavy flowery scent he'd smelt when he'd opened the envelope. They'd all pointed to someone a bit special.

But even so, he'd never in a million years have imagined her as special as this. With hair like a living flame; dark, hungry eyes; and a red-stained, supermodel mouth. Mrs Caspell's 'look' was both chic and outrageous. She wore crimson leather from throat to toe: a boxy, wide-shouldered jacket, a skimpy bra top, and a short, tight skirt. She was sitting down, but Jem guessed she was tall, and made all the more so by high, spiked-heeled shoes in the same red leather as her clothes. What he was looking at was a total fantasy, an archetype, a woman who was beyond his wildest longings, yet living, sensual and vibrant. He'd only seen her fifteen seconds ago, but already his young cock felt as hard as a poker.

Cursing his nerves and his randiness, he swallowed hard, then strode across the foyer. Aquake inside, he held out the single scarlet rose he'd brought her, then told the apparition his name: Jem. The rose had been a daft impulse but, crazily enough, it worked. Mrs Caspell sighed softly, then smiled with a unfeigned pleasure and gestured Jem to sit down. Heads turned all across the foyer when she leant across and kissed him on the lips with a pressure that was slow and inquisitive.

When she broke away, Jem still couldn't speak. Stunned, he listened to her charming and poised introduction, and her thanks for his recent good deed. His heart went 'boing' inside him as she said his nickname, her soft voice husky and breathy.

Oh, shit, she'll think I'm an moron! he thought, hating his disabling shyness. Tongue-tied, he tried to focus on the one thing he did have going for him: his looks. He might be a stuttering nerd at times like this, but at least he was easy on the eye. His hair was thick, dark-brown and shiny. His skin was smooth and blemish-free, and his features were almost classical – large hazel-gold eyes, lips that were full, firm and sculpted.

In spite of his stupid misconception about Mrs Caspell being fair, fat and forty, he'd still dressed with the intention of impressing her. His suit was a pale biscuit colour and his shirt and tie two shades darker. It was only cheap chainstore gear, and the suit was second-hand, but with a bit of care and attention, he could wear it and feel he looked sharp. In the midst of Jem's sartorial ditherings, a waiter appeared. Swiftly and politely, the man placed a bottle and two glasses on the low table before them, and was gone again in an instant. Mrs Caspell poured the wine herself, skilfully filling each glass without spilling a single drop.

Jem took his drink and tasted it cautiously. It was a fantastic vintage he was sure, but he wasn't in fit state to enjoy it. He was dizzy and light-headed already; his heart pounding, his stomach fluttering, and inside his best, and only pair of pure silk boxer shorts, his prick was so hard it was hurting! Nearly sick with desire, he put his glass down and edged closer to the woman beside him. Then, without stopping to ask, or even think, he slid his arm around her sleek, narrow waist.

What the hell am I doing? he asked himself, shocked by the rashness of this move. He almost leapt clean out of his skin when Mrs Caspell smiled in approval, went 'Mmm', and moved in tight against his body. Almost dreamily, he stroked her smooth, bare midriff, and wondered if he'd ever be able to speak. It was hard to believe he'd thought meeting this woman would be a chore, but still he couldn't relax. Raw, white need raced through him, its painful flames stoked by her fingers. Long and graceful, they felt like thistledown wherever they touched him; questing slowly from his forearm to his thigh, and making his skin burn like fire beneath his suit.

They were supposed to be having dinner soon,

but Mrs Caspell seemed to be in no hurry. 'Let's freshen up in my suite first, shall we?' she murmured, squeezing his leg. As she led the way towards the lift, her perfect bottom swaying like a salsa, a light went on in Jem's brain. It suddenly dawned on him what 'profound appreciation' might mean.

It couldn't be true! 'The older woman' was his all-time, ultimate masturbation fantasy; the dream of his nineteen-year-old life. And it was happening here and now for real.

'Jem,' she murmured as the lift door closed.

His name seemed to fall from her dewy, red lips and settle on his prick like a moth. A single, simple syllable, it acquired an almost physical substance – a resonance. It coiled around his prick like wet silk and then danced along his whole twitching length. 'Jem,' she whispered again, then slid into his arms and made him hers.

This time it was Jem who did the kissing. Mrs Caspell's mouth opened wide beneath his, inviting him to drink from its moistness. His tongue dove in deep as she moulded her body to his, and like a lost boy he rubbed himself against her. Then stopped dead.

Oh God, his hard-on! He tried to pull back but Mrs Caspell wouldn't let him. Locking her hands in the small of his back, she worked her pelvis to and fro against his, massaging the thick bulge of his cock with the curve of her leather-covered belly.

In her suite the kiss continued. Jem had never wanted any woman as much as this, and quite obviously, she wanted him too. There was lust in the air all around them, but in a low seductive whisper, Mrs Caspell insisted they slow down and pace themselves. 'The longer the wait, the sweeter the fuck,' she promised, her mouth moving softly on his neck.

Jem nearly came on the spot. He'd heard women swear before, plenty of times, but he'd never heard one so beautfiul say 'fuck'.

But shock piled on shock. With a deftness that left him reeling, Mrs Caspell unzipped his fly, flicked open his boxer shorts, and eased out his heavy young cock. He yelped out aloud as she fingered his hard flesh: assessing the thickness and the weight of it, and scrutinising its long jutting shape.

How on earth could she think of waiting? Jem felt his entire body gather itself to plunge. He wanted to tip her on to the bed, bear down on her and tear off skirt and her panties. She'd be ready, he could tell. He didn't have all that much experience, but he knew she'd be wet, lush and open. Almost beside himself, he lurched forward – but Mrs Caspell only shook her head, tut-tutted, then tucked his penis back into his shorts. As she zipped him up, he was torn between relief and unbearable frustration. He'd been terrified of coming in her hand; yet her touch was so divine he could've wept. Without thinking, he gasped the word 'please'.

'Don't worry, Jem.' Her smile was slight and tantalising. 'It'll be soon. But first we've got to build up your strength.'

Their dinner was magnificent – doubly so when a four-course square meal was so rare for him – but Jem barely tasted a thing.

It was Mrs Caspell that *he* hungered for. His entire groin felt swollen and bloated, and he could do nothing but grit his teeth, and hold on grimly; waiting for the moment when she set him free from his stiffness and his misery. When she pressed her napkin to her tinted mouth and decreed that the meal was over, he sighed out loud with relief; then looked away from her low sultry laugh.

When they entered the suite, Mrs Caspell excused herself immediately and left Jem alone with his erection. He decided to follow her example and 'freshen up' in the second of the suite's ritzy bathrooms.

Fifteen minutes later, he returned to the bedroom, naked, harder than ever, and very nervous. Mrs Caspell was still 'freshening', but he could see she'd returned to the room in his absence.

The bedlinen had been meticulously turned down, and the pristine white area at 'his' side exposed. Mrs Caspell's attention to detail was strangely exciting and Jem's cock twitched at the thought of it. Was she this thorough in her lovemaking?

The only trouble was . . . in this situation there was one detail *he* should've attended to.

It would never have occured to Jem in a million years that he'd end up in bed tonight, so consequently he'd not brought protection. Anxiety started to wilt him, but as he looked around his eye lit on a sight that made him sigh with relief. Mrs Caspell had left a discreet but familiar box on the bedside table. A box with its lid flipped open to show the small silver packages within.

Jem prised out a condom, and studied its slim, distinctive shape. His free hand drifted automatically to his cock, and he felt a jolt of sensation in his loins. In his imagination, his searching fingers became Mrs Caspell's – examining him neatly and surely as she rolled down the skin-sheer rubber over his raging, ruby-tipped shaft.

Biting his lip, he abandoned his prick and tried to calm down. 'Cool it, Jem,' he admonished in a whisper. 'You haven't even seen her naked yet.'

Sliding on to the bed, he pulled the sheet up over him and savoured its smooth texture on his skin. The comfort and opulence of the room seemed just as much a fantasy as Mrs Caspell herself was, but as he lay there, his thoughts took a bizarre new turn.

By all that was natural and normal, he should be imagining Mrs Caspell's unclothed body now, but suddenly he saw the broad, grinning face of the bobby who'd taken in the pendant. The laughing policeman with his eyes that were salacious and knowing. 'Jammy young bastard' the man had mouthed – as if he'd seen the future and this very moment.

Suddenly, there was a small sound somewhere to Jem's right. Hardly breathing, he turned his head slowly on the pillow.

Swathed in what looked like cobwebs of creamy silk lace, Mrs Caspell was walking, almost floating towards him. When she reached the bedside, she eyed him speculatively, then shrugged her shoulders and let her soft, filmy garment fall away.

Jem felt like crying again, and this time, to his horror, it really happened. The woman before him was perfect. His complete, fully functioning dream. Her body was mature, yet delicate and slim; her skin was immaculate; her large, rounded breasts were crowned with the pinkest of nipples that were exquisitely puckered and stiff. At the apex of her long, sleek thighs, she had hair that was silky, lush and thick, a bouquet of blondish-red curls.

Jem blinked furiously to clear his tears. She was all he'd ever wanted, everything he'd ever yearned for. His problems seemed to fall away like mist, as if just one night with this fabulous woman might sustain him for months, even years to come. He lay completely still and passive while she threw back the sheets, climbed on to the bed, and knelt beside him.

At first, she just studied him, her eyes glittering and dark. Then she started touching him, exploring with her long, tapered fingers and praising every feature she encountered. She enthused at length about his strong young physique, his smooth skin, and his hair. She admired his neck, his arms, his thighs and his hard, flat belly.

But when she reached his aching, straining cock, she seemed to find a whole new vocabulary, describing it with a eloquent lyricism, and an earthy and full-bodied directness.

Jem was stunned. He'd jumped a mile when she'd said 'Fuck' – and now she was saying ... saying everything! But it sounded more like poetry than a description of a man's naked body.

When the inventory was over, Mrs Caspell lay back and flexed herself slowly like a cat.

'Would you like to make love to me, Jem?' she asked. Her voice was calm and quiet, yet her question felt more like an order.

Obediently, he began kissing and licking her breasts and she hissed 'yes!' between her teeth in approval. After a moment, she whispered that he should bite her nipples, and he complied just as quickly, without question.

As his teeth closed lightly on her teat, he felt her pushing his hand to her cunt. Guiding him to a place that was already wet, and as molten as a furnace. A place where he first dabbled tentatively, then probed with more fervour, rubbing at the pearl of her clitoris.

Jem's caresses were blind guesswork, but happily they seemed to be the right ones. Mrs Caspell whimpered and squirmed as he suckled at her breast, her hips rising keenly to his touch. After a moment, she stilled, then jerked once, twice, three times in his arms, sobbing long and loud as her body thrashed and turned in its climax. Jem could hardly breathe or think. His only awareness was feeling. The tip of his manhood . . . Beneath it, satin flesh jumping madly.

Everything went quiet for a while, then Mrs Caspell started pushing at his head. With both hands, she urged him imperiously downwards, and Jem trembled when his lips met her belly.

As he kissed her smooth, white skin, he found a tiny scar just below her navel. Tracing its shape with his tongue, he wondered what'd happened there, and hoped it hadn't been too painful. When he moved lower, and nuzzled at her thick pubic floss, she generously drew apart her thighs and showed him her rosy female treasure.

Just inches from his nose, Jem saw curlicues of ruffled, swollen flesh, and a landscape that was glistening with her juices. At its heart was the minute, mysterious portal that would soon expand to receive him, and sliding his hands gently beneath her, he lifted up her body to his mouth and put his tongue to the membranes of her sex. She rippled like a wave as he licked her, and when he stabbed hard and quickly at her clitoris, she cried out in an extremity of pleasure.

Mrs Caspell wriggled and heaved but Jem held on tight. His tongue rode her deep, moist valley and he felt a great, almost terrible excitement. Her taste was rich and pungent, and her nectar flowed freely across his face, smearing his cheeks and his chin as her body arched up from the bed. He furled his tongue-tip, stabbed again, and her shouts turned to harsh, ragged screams. She was incoherent, but he didn't need words. He sensed her whirling on some hidden, inner fulcrum, lost in a free-soaring orgasm as her body throbbed and leapt against his mouth.

When Mrs Caspell's eyes fluttered open, she smiled radiantly and Jem knew he'd not been found wanting. He'd been tested, yes, but he'd passed, and passed well. Stroking his sweaty hair, Mrs Caspell whispered that it was 'his turn now' and with his desire for her racing through his veins. Jem rolled over on to his back in readiness.

Then blushed like a shoolboy.

His prick was standing straight up from his groin, stiffer than ever and waving very slightly in the air. The head of it was red and distended and pre-come ran out thickly from the tip. Tossing back her touseled red hair, Mrs Caspell hunched over him, and lowered her soft lips to his flesh.

Incredible!

Her mouth was a sucking well of heat, a hot liquid sheath that enclosed him in a way he'd only dreamed of. He felt engulfed by her, consumed by her, his penis both devoured and renewed.

She held him like that for long, long seconds, then relaxed her lips and took him in deeper. Deeper and unbelievably deeper, traversing his whole contained length with the tip of her amazing wet tongue.

It was like floating on a raft of sheer bliss, and Mrs Caspell's oral skills seemed boundless. One minute, she'd graze him with her small white teeth, the next, she'd hollow her cheeks and suck like fury until Jem thought his brain would explode. Teasing without mercy, she backed off again and again – just before the point of no return – leaving him balanced on an edge so critical that he pleaded and begged for release. Shouting mindless gibberish, he stared down from a mountaintop of rarefied sensation at the wildest, and most colourful of sights. A pair of glossy-painted red-stained lips sliding slowly on his purple-veined cock.

As her mouth worked, so did her fingers: stroking his thighs, jiggling his balls, dipping down into the cleft of his buttocks to tickle at his dark little opening. When she touched him there, Jem's eyes bulged. He bucked like a bronco on the bed and almost threw Mrs Caspell off his crotch!

After what seemed like a millenium, she planted one last kiss on the fat pink tip of his prick and licked up its round pearl of juice. Then she slid back on to the bed at his side, threw open her long, pale thighs, and pulled his body determinedly towards her.

The transition between suck and fuck was effortless. Even his usual disaster area – getting the condom on – was as smooth and co-ordinated as a dance. Between them, he and Mrs Caspell encased him in the microfine sleeve, then with a single guiding touch of her fingers, he plunged to his utmost inside her, and lodged deep in her moist clinging vale. As he plumbed her, he held his breath, scared that even a sigh might dissolve his perfect dream. But when Mrs Caspell gasped voluptuously beneath him, the fantasy stayed solid around them, and he felt her breath like a zephyr on his neck.

Her flesh was like hot liquid velvet, with an inner grip so snug and form-fitting that their bodies seemed machined to fit each other. Entranced, Jem just lay there and let Mrs Caspell – his goddess – work her magic. He felt her hands settle softly on his back, then slide lower and cup the cheeks of his bottom. As her fingers kneaded and pounded him, she started rocking her pelvis to their rhythm –

creating a pleasure for herself out of his. Jem wanted to shaft her like a madman, fuck her like an animal, but somehow he managed to restrict himself, using slow, measured shoves that steadied his race towards climax.

But not, alas, for very long. It was their first time together, and Mrs Caspell was his ultimate and definitive dream. The faster he plunged inside her, the more she rose to meet him – a challenge for his every frenzied stroke.

She's fucking *me!* Jem thought in wonder, breathing hard against her sweat-sheened neck. He felt her juddering and contracting around him, and like a comet wreathed in white fire and glory, his climax roared towards him from the heavens.

When it arrived, Mrs Caspell made it welcome. 'Fuck me! Oh God, fuck me! I'm coming!' she shouted as she writhed beneath his weight.

And fuck her he did. Thrusting in with all his young strength, he matched her fierce cry with his own.

'Anna!' he screamed, as a heavy, beating pulse fluttered wildly in the warm depths that held him.

Jem couldn't tell whether the rhythm came from Anna's flesh or his – he didn't care. Their ecstasy had made them into one . . .

Sunshine was streaming into the room when Jem woke up, but it wasn't the light that'd roused him. Blinking and scrabbling around sleepily, he realised to his sorrow that he was alone. Mrs Caspell had gone, and left only her sweet perfume to console him.

'No!' he cried, sitting up, his heart a cold empty void.

When had she left? Where had she gone? Could

he catch her if he ran outside now? Naked . . .

What would happen to him, he wondered, if he didn't find her? One night with Mrs Caspell had been more reward that he could ever have hoped for, but suddenly it wasn't enough. 'No!' he shouted again, then froze with the words on his lips.

On the pillow next to his – in the dent where his darling had slept – was an object that was small, pink and square: a sheet of writing paper, folded in a neat little package. Shaking like a leaf, Jem picked it up, and as he unfolded it, out fell her pretty black pendant.

Dearest Jem, said the flamboyant, looping script.

> *You can keep this now. I shan't need to 'lose' it anymore, because I've found what I wanted.*
>
> *Sell it if you like. Buy some new clothes . . . You'll need them. I'll be in touch with you later today, and we can discuss a more permanent arrangement.*

> *Yours,*

> *Anna*

Yelling and laughing like a fool, Jem leapt out of bed and raced at top speed for the shower. Once in it, he started soaping his smooth body jubilantly, and working up a rich frothing lather – especially around his newly-hardened penis.

As he rubbed, he thought of the black heart, the pink note, and the angel who'd left them beside him. 'Finders keepers, Mrs Caspell,' he gasped, as his semen spurted thickly in her honour. 'And if you want to, you can keep *me* forever!'

Condition Orange

IF YOU'RE SHY, DON'T APPLY!
Wanted: stylish young man with good body for
undraped studies. Excellent remuneration. Apply
– with recent photograph – to Miranda Scott, Box
No. 1717.

Pip ran his finger around the rim of his glass, and
wondered what a lady photographer might look
like. Over the last few hours he'd pinned a hundred
different faces to her voice – but he didn't think any
one of them was right. She sounded sexy, but there
was an edge in there somewhere, an emotion he
couldn't quite define. Perplexed, he considered a
second drink, and wondered what *she'd* think of
him. Obviously the polaroid he'd sent had made a
good impression – she must've phoned him within
minutes of receiving it. But the photo had been
taken for a giggle, at a party, what she'd think of the
real Pip was debatable.

He was a young man of medium height – a dark
young man. He had dark hair, dark eyes, and dark
skin. His slightly swarthy skin was a legacy from his
beautiful Lebanese grandmother, and a casual

summer work as a gardener meant he was the same toasted brown all over. Even the naughtier bits had been evened out in seclusion, but for this job he wished his physique was more developed and chunkier. Still, Ms Scott must've liked what she'd seen; and as he adjusted his behind on the bar-stool, and felt his orange alert turning into red, Pip wondered if she fancied his cock. It *was* a good long size, he reflected, and it had been standing up in the picture.

It was trying to stand up now, but for photography that could be a problem. He was aware of certain laws about the condition of a male pin-up's penis, and he didn't think his present state complied. Perhaps he'd better have another drink and hope that alcohol would make his stalk droop.

He was just about to signal for the barman when the back of his neck prickled strangely. He didn't exactly know how he knew it, but Miranda, the photographer, was here.

But when he turned around, he nearly fell off his stool. Miranda Scott was indeed quite unlike any preconceived picture he'd formed. She wasn't arty, she wasn't 'media' and she wasn't even carrying a camera. What she did have, beneath her leather encased arm, was a shiny-black motorcycle helmet. His photographer was a 'hell's angelette'!

Dressed in black leathers from head to foot, Miranda was leanly-built woman of medium height, and of an age he couldn't put his finger on. As Pip watched, transfixed, she pulled off her butch looking gauntlets and ran her fingers through her slickly-cropped, tawny-coloured hair.

'Er . . . Hi,' he answered at last, dropping down on to his feet as he remembered that it was customary to stand for a lady, even if she was one of the least ladylike he'd ever seen.

'I'm Philip Taylor-Kay,' he stammered, holding out his hand, 'My friends call me "Pip" . . . and you must be Ms Scott?'

'Call me "Scottie".' She took his hand in one that was still warm from her glove. 'That's with an "i" and an "e" by the way. I'm pleased to meet you.'

He tried to meet her eyes, but found it difficult. Hers were cool and steel-grey, their chilliness at odds with her heated skin. He felt that peculiar tingle again, the frisson he'd felt just minutes ago, but it faded when she smiled at him amenably.

'Would you like a drink?' he asked, feeling he should at least make an effort to get to know her. Somehow, though, this 'Scottie' didn't look like a someone who wasted time on meaningless pleasantries. 'Thanks, but no thanks,' she said crisply, stuffing her gloves into her pocket and whizzing down her jacket's hefty zip, 'I've got a bottle of gin in my room . . . Why don't we go up and get to work?'

'Er, yes . . . Fine . . .'

He was already following her as he spoke, still stunned by a momentary vision. The sight of a tender, dark-tipped cone beneath thin white cotton. For just a second, as she'd turned, he'd seen the body beneath the jacket, and a bra-less breast beneath the ultra-thin cloth of a T-shirt.

Scottie said little in the lift and Pip was glad of it. He didn't feel capable of conversation, and Scottie didn't have to speak anyway. Her body had its own unique language.

She stood with a straight back and her legs apart and braced, a stance that added inches to her height. To Pip she was utterly beautiful, just his type. She was the hard bitch; the amazon. Like the girl in *Terminator Two*, or Ripley, the Alien's adversary. She wouldn't flutter or flirt, or play silly girl games, yet she wore a brilliant Russian Red lipstick on a mouth that clearly meant business. He wanted her so much he was aching.

As she let him into her room, it occurred to Pip that this was a rather odd location for a shoot. Didn't photographers work in studios with spotlights and backdrops? But when she shucked of her tough, leather jacket, and abandoned her helmet, all questions dissolved like a mist.

What he'd thought was a T-shirt was in fact a skimpy white vest and her figure was more curvy than he'd expected. Her arms and shoulders were wiry, but her breasts were rounded and high, her waist narrow, and her hips had a soft sweet flare. Her legs looked almost endless in their glistening leather carapace and the double stitched line of her fly seemed to signpost the direction of heaven.

'Make yourself useful then,' she said, raising an eyebrow at his dithering silence. 'Fix us both a drink.' She nodded in the direction of the mini-bar, and the green litre bottle that stood on top of it. 'Mine's straight gin. You can please yourself, there's plenty to choose from in there.'

As he fiddled with glasses and ice, Pip watched her make the room into a studio. In a few mintues, she had fluffy white towels spread all over the bed and its headboard; and around that, at carefully paced out distances, she set a number of small, directable lights. On an occasional table she laid out an impressive selection of cameras.

The bed was now an intimidating zone of radiance, a hard white circle that made Pip dry-mouthed and nervous. At any moment, he'd have to shed his clothes before Scottie – and reveal to her his stone-hard erection.

He'd not intended to have another drink, but now he needed one. He didn't like gin but he poured himself some anyway. It smelt silvery and resinous, and to disguise its distinctive flavour he rummaged in the mini-bar, found a small can of orange juice, and topped up his glass with that.

'Orange . . . Hmm?' murmured Scottie, looking up from her viewfinder. 'Good idea. Sloosh some into my glass too, will you?'

As he passed the drink across, Pip caught a strange expression on her face. For an instant, she appeared deeply unhappy. Sad, but wry too. Resigned; as if she were trapped in some cycle of sorrow that no amount of attitude could break.

'Cheers!' she murmured, her voice light and neutral as she tapped her full glass against his. 'Let's get to work, shall we? We'll start with a few shots *avec* clothes and work our way down to the skin.'

The modelling, when it came, was easy. Pip was amazed. He stood against the bed, he sat and he lay on it, and felt so comfortable he forgot his erection. It was only when Scottie touched him there – and he nearly shot through the roof with the pleasure of it – that he remembered the problem of his stiffness.

'Very nice,' she murmured softly, her fingertips lingering while Pip just shook. 'Shall we get a little closer to it?'

In an instant she was peeling off his clothes. First, she knelt down to remove his shoes and socks – her brow on a level with the swelling bulge in his chainstore Armani trousers – then she rose again to ease off his jacket. Pip stood still, a frozen mannequin, his arms moving limply at her bidding. He felt completely helpless, undermined in a way he'd never been before. He was rampant, yet unmanned by her slight, strong body and her sharp, very feminine fragrance – a pine soap, and something more musky; something quite basic and female, the hot distinctive smell of her natural scent.

Did she want him? Did his emerging young body arouse her? It was difficult to tell because she seemed so focused – but her nipples were pushing hard through her vest, and they seemed darker then they'd looked to him before.

The next pose was blatantly sexual. She made him lie on the bed, one hand inside his half unbuttoned shirt and the other lying draped across his groin. As she fiddled with her camera, and made the final adjustments to her lighting, he could feel his cock hot and throbbing through his trousers. He tried not to press down and stroke himself, but there was a riot in the hard flesh beneath; a craving. His 'condition orange' was a full red alert now, and he had a terrible, precognition that long before the rest of his clothes came off, his body would erupt and betray him. Every snap, snap, snap of her shutter seemed to impact directly on his penis.

She took another long sequence of shots, and then, to rearrange his limbs more precisely, she climbed on to the bed with him – and for this she kicked off her boots. Her white cotton socks were as innocent as a schoolgirl's, and for some indefinable reason the sight of them made Pip's cock leap. He could hardly keep still. He wanted to bend down, peel off those dainty white socks, then press his lips to her soft, slender feet.

'Right, Pip, take your clothes off and let's go for it,' she said suddenly, her voice no longer so controlled and silky. As she stepped off the bed, she appeared – for an instant – to sway.

Under any other circumstances, Pip would've leapt to her aid, worried about that moment of weakness and the strange, sad look that haunted her; but now all he could feel was an intense, excited embarrassment. His cock felt huge to him, enormous. It might please her; or she might be furious, because his stiffness would ruin her pictures.

Tentatively, he slipped off his shirt, and tossed it aside, then fumbled with the buckle on his belt. After a few seconds it yielded, but already there was sweat beneath armpits and a hot flush rising up his throat.

'Don't worry . . . Take your time,' said Scottie. She sounded calm, but there was noticeable hardening of her nipples and pinkness on her smooth, pale cheeks. She was breathing more heavily too, her small breasts rising and falling beneath the cling of the thin white vest. Perspiration was visible at her hairline, the slick of it shining on her throat.

As he stood up, and slid down his trousers, he modestly turned his back. With his fingers poised in the waistband of his briefs, he sensed her studying the shape of his buttocks, her eyes casting heat across his cleft.

'Come on, don't be coy . . . I want to oil you.'

'Oil?' he asked blankly.

'An essential ingredient in skin shots, Pip, my dear,' she purred, a rich sensuality replacing the transitory impression of ennui. There were several plastic bottles already on the coffee table, and a porcelain bowl, and as he watched her, she began pouring and mixing. 'Pants off, please,' she said emphatically, nodding at his skimpy tan briefs and the gross bulge distending the front of them.

When he tugged off his knickers, his erection bounced up like a sapling, its tip reaching out to Scottie. 'Is . . . is this a problem?' he asked, glancing downwards. He was felt like a horny adolescent caught wanking, but bizarrely it only made him harder.

'Not in the slightest,' she answered, still blending. 'A big stiff prick is an asset. I don't shoot for commercial circulation . . . so anything and everything goes.'

His disappointment must've shown on his face. He was unemployed and he'd been anticipating the 'big break'.

'Don't worry. I'll mention your name in the right places.' Absorbed, she ignored both his face and his frisky erection. She was busy measuring out a minute amount of a substance from a smaller, brown bottle. When she was satisfied with her quantities, she swirled her potion with a flourish; even from halfway across the room, Pip could instantly smell its aroma.

The fragrance was sharp, sweet, deliciously and voluptuously fruity. It seemed to flow straight in through his pores, and caress both his heart and his gonads. He felt mellow, marvellously warm; his spirit at peace and his shyness a long-forgotten memory. He shivered with a deep erotic anticipation as Scottie approached him with her bowl, then trickled its contents on his chest. As the oil oozed slowly across his pectorals, she started spreading it and kneading with her fingers.

'What's in it?' he murmured, closing his eyes, not embarrassed now, but suffused with a lovely relaxation. Her fingertips moved strongly but were also exquisitely gentle, their action setting fire to the fragrance. 'I can smell fruit,' he said breathing deeply and almost floating away.

'The carrier is a mix of almond, wheatgerm and walnut, but the ingredient you can smell is orange oil. Pure and essential . . . Fruit for the brain.'

'Smells fabulous,' Pip murmured, shimmying helplessly as she sleeked the oil in long, efficient strokes across his ribcage and belly, then spread it out tormentingly over the creases of his groin and his thighs – avoiding his cock completely. In a ferment, he wondered what orange would do to him there. But he found out almost immediately when Scottie recharged her hands with oil and gently took hold of his stiffness. 'Oh God,' he whispered as her fingers slithered and slid, and his flesh seemed to swell and tingle. 'If that's what orange oil does for you, please, give me more!'

'Orange oil,' she intoned, her fingers still skilfully pumping him as she began a list of the oil's sovereign attributes. 'Good for skin conditioning, for relaxation, for muscular aches and pains . . .' She paused then, delicately caressing the tip of him, and when she spoke again her voice was sombre, 'Orange oil . . . Beneficial also for depression, hopelessness and lack of joy.'

The bleakness of her words seemed to fracture his drifting euphoria. Puzzled, he looked up, then said the first thing that came into his head. 'But I'm not depressed. I'm having a great time!'

'It's for me, Pip,' she said grimly, 'and don't ask why because it's too complicated.'

He persisted. 'Why? Why do you need it?'

She seemed not to hear him. Abandoning his long swaying penis, she stood up purposefully, wiped her hands on a towel and reached for one of her cameras. 'To work now, Pip . . . Let's do it!' Her spirits had obviously lifted and her movements were neat and animated, but there was still a faint shadow in her eyes.

The poses that followed were outrageous and made Pip forget all his questions. In a thick miasma

71

of orange, she arranged his body into shapes that would formerly have shocked him, and placed his hands on his flesh in ways he'd never have placed them himself. One half of him cringed, thinking of the images they were creating, while the other half quivered with pleasure. When she quietly ordered him to climax, he obeyed in an ecstasy of willingness.

Through the confusion of his own release, he sensed that Scottie too was gradually growing more sensitised. When she finally laid down her cameras, he was shocked that she didn't invite him to kiss her. He'd been so sure she wanted his body; so sure that they'd end up making love.

'But Scottie,' he protested as she started to stow away her gear. 'What happens now?'

'You get dressed. I pay you. You leave,' she said flatly.

'But what do you do?'

She paused again, her body quite still, her pale face washed of emotion.

'I put away my equipment. I masturbate. Then I leave.'

It sounded so stark and soulless, and Pip's body tightened with anger. Somewhere in the oil's soporific sweetness was an element that also sharpened the senses. Without knowing why or quite how, he knew that someone had hurt her; crippled her need for people; detached her in a private world of warped and sterile pleasure. It was obvious that she used the powerful effects of odours to help her fight her malaise, but he saw now she couldn't prevail – not on her own.

'Let me do it,' he said, rising from the bed, his naked thighs sliding with the oil. His cock was already resurrecting.

'Do what?' Her grey eyes were narrow and he sensed the stark damage inside her.

'Let me touch you. Give you your joy . . . Please, let me try?'

'Why should I? When I've paid you I don't owe you anything.' She was reaching for her jacket now, and presumably her wallet or chequebook.

'Why?' he mused, the citrus odour still at work on his spirits and his cock. 'Well, because I want some joy, and I don't think I can get it from anybody but you.' He was in front of her now, his hands and his penis reaching out. 'Please, Scottie, please! Forget my fee! Just let me stay here and touch you.'

'What the hell,' she said her voice still heavy yet carrying just the slightest spark of hope. With a small fated sigh, she leaned in towards him, pressed her breasts to his hard oily chest and encircled his waist with her arms. 'What've I got to lose . . . Let's fuck!'

Pip remember those words the next morning as he awoke in her bed and alone.

It hadn't been an easy task, bringing Scottie to joy. She'd been wary and tense, almost impossible to soften and please. But he'd persevered, smeared her body with warmed oil from his, and eventually he'd broken through her barriers. With a fund of patience and skill he hadn't even known he'd possessed, he made her sob and writhe, then jerk wildly in a hard-won climax.

After that they'd flowed together more smoothly and Scottie had relaxed and smiled – and come again on his fingers and his tongue.

He'd hoped against hope that it'd all meant something to her, but somehow her absence this morning was no real surprise. Especially not after what he'd discovered while she was showering and he'd got up to nose around . . .

It was all down to the orange and the gin, he thought bitterly. Just a fantasy, an essential oil trip.

In low spirits, he washed away the last trances of citrus from his body and dejectedly climbed into his clothes. She'd left his money, plus a massive tip, on the pillow, but knowing what he did now, the cash only made him feel sleazy. He wished she'd left him the orange oil instead.

Nobody seemed to take any notice of him in the hotel foyer, a young man in last night's crumpled suit. He put his head down, walked straight ahead . . . and was just about to step into the revolving door when Scottie stepped out of it, a newspaper in one hand and a twirling set of keys in the other.

'Where the hell are you going?' Her voice was angry, but in her deep grey eyes there was fear. And hurt. And an almost choking disappointment.

Pip froze. He'd made a huge mistake. A gigantic one. Not last night, but this morning.

'I thought that was it,' he said quietly, while his heart screamed at Scottie to listen. 'I saw the money and all your stuff gone. I thought you'd gone too.'

'I only went to stow my gear in my panniers, and get a paper. I was coming back to take you to breakfast.' She was starting to smile now, and her pale face was brightening and warming. 'I thought we might discuss another shoot . . . or several.'

Pip didn't want breakfast. He was hungry, but not for eggs or toast. Wasting no time on speech, he took a step forward, put his lips against hers, and used the pressure of his hands on her leather-covered bottom to pull her close and let her know what he needed.

'Scottie, you know the next time we "shoot",' he

began as their mouths drew apart.

Should he mention it? Let her know that he knew? He decided 'Yes' – because honesty was the best base to build on. 'The next time, do you think you could actually put some film in the camera?'

For several long moments her face remained blank and expressionless, and Pip was thrown back to a time beyond confidence, beyond pleasure, beyond nakedness and pure orange oil. But then she laughed – and laughed and laughed – her sleek head falling backwards as she chortled. He'd discovered her sly, kinky secret, but happily it didn't seem to matter. 'Okay, then, just for you.' She leaned close again and kissed his cheek, then smiled archly, her power back on line. 'Now, shall we eat?'

As they walked arm in arm towards the dining room, she seemed to muse a moment, then turned to him. 'I think we'll try a different oil next time too,' she said, her voice so much softer and more resonant. 'I might not need orange any more.'

Pip knew she wouldn't need orange oil, but as he escorted Scottie proudly to their table, he seemed to smell the faint ghost of it anyway . . .

A round, sweet fragrance, fruity and revivifying, the ineffable aroma of joy.

Crème de la Crème

'WHAT SORT OF fantasies do you have, Pandora?'

Jake Mallinson cursed inwardly at his perennial and insatiable curiosity. It was probably going to screw up his chances with the most interesting woman he'd met in ages!

'Mine? What on earth do you want to know about *my* fantasies for?' Pandora studied him obliquely across the outlandish sketch she'd just drawn. 'It's yours that're important . . . You're the one who's paying for this.' She tapped the paper before them for emphasis.

'Yes, I know that.'

Jake thought furiously. How could he prise her secrets from her? He had to know more – she was driving him crazy! 'But I thought I might get some sexy new ideas from you,' he improvised, 'for the apartment, that is . . . You're the interior designer, Pandora. You're the one with the creative mind.'

And the delicious body! he added silently, eyeing her elegant curves and the way her clothes hugged them so faithfully.

She'd changed her outfit since earlier in the day– when they'd surveyed his new flat – and was now wrapped in chic off-white from top to toe. A fine cream sweater shaped to her high, rounded breasts and a pair of milky, jeans-cut trousers embraced the contours of her legs and hips. This was the first time Jake had gotten a close look at Pandora's opulent undercarriage, and he'd discovered she was no less delightful below than above. Her hips were womanly yet lithe, and her backside pure heaven: tight, muscular and utterly curvy. For perhaps the hundredth time, he considered the mysterious vee of her groin, and wished his fingers were beneath that tantalising, double-stitched seam. His mind flashed back to one of his own recent fantasies – the lady rubbing herself madly for his amusement – and the picture was so graphically clear that he nearly came right there in his shorts.

Did Pandora masturbate? She was a healthy, vibrantly sensual woman who often worked closely with men. Surely she had a strong sex-drive? Surely that drive needed satisfying?

An uncomfortable thought suddenly occurred. Maybe Pandora was refusing his non-professional approaches because she was already involved? Because she was getting regular sex with somebody else?

'Maybe you don't need to fantasise,' he ventured.

'And what do you mean by that?'

'Well . . . If you've got a boyfriend and he's giving you plenty, you won't need to dream about it, will you?'

'Who'd go out with me?' She turned slowly in her seat, then nodded towards the substantial-looking hickory walking-stick that was propped discreetly against the bar. There was a bitterness in her beautiful eyes, and Jake realised that although he'd clean forgotten her infirmity, it was impossible for her to do the same.

'I would!'

He tried to put something more than desire in his voice. He'd only known her a few days yet he wanted to . . . he wanted . . .

What the hell did he want? He did physically lust for Pandora Jackson. More perhaps than for any woman ever. But half-hearted as it sounded, he also wanted to be her friend. His own occasional feelings of isolation were bad enough, but how much more 'different' must Pandora feel when she so obviously considered herself flawed?

'Jake! We've covered all that ground already—'

'Okay! Okay! Okay! I'll leave it. But I'm still interested in your fantasies.'

'All right then, although I can't think why I'm telling you,' she said slowly, then paused to take a sip of her drink. 'I only came here to discuss the commission. And anyway . . . you'll be grossly disappointed, I can tell you that for a start!'

'No way!'

'Don't be so sure. My fantasies are old-fashioned, Jake. And boringly conventional.' She shrugged dismissively. 'I like romance: soft lights, lingerie, sipping champagne. A man who's gentle and gentlemanly; who'd treat me like a lady . . . A man who'd treat me as if *this* didn't exist!' She touched her leg, the one that was stretched out awkwardly, and not as straight and relaxed as the other.

Jake moved uncomfortably. He was ashamed to say that all he could think of was what was *between* her legs, not the legs themselves. 'But surely they can fix it?' he asked in an attempt to distract himself. After all, with orthopaedic surgery being so miraculous these days, she shouldn't really have to stay lame.

'You don't understand, Jake, do you? This is "after", not "before". They've fixed me up as much as they could. I've had umpteen bonegrafts. I've got a dozen steel pins in my thigh. I nearly lost the whole bloody leg!' She patted the stiffened limb which looked quite slender, shapely and normal in her elegant, flattering trousers. 'This is the best it gets. Ever . . .'

But it shouldn't matter, thought Jake, soaping his own sound, unblemished body. He was in the shower now, in his hotel suite. Though it was over two hours later, he was still brooding about Pandora, her dreams, her untreatable leg, and the lack of men who'd look beyond a slight but strangely appealing limp and see a truly remarkable woman. He couldn't believe he was the only one to whom it didn't matter? The problem, he suspected, was bedded in Pandora's own mind. She questioned her own sex appeal, and Jake wondered if someone had let her down.

'But not me, lady!' he proclaimed aloud in her absence.

I wouldn't let you down, he told her across the gulf of the glittering city. I'd treat you like a queen. If you'd give me half a chance – or even a quarter! – I'd lavish you with all the romance and tender loving care you can handle. And then some!

Under the teeming shower, through the steam and pine-scented foam, Jake let Pandora's sweet dream become his.

He saw her boudoir, self-designed in a romantically antique style, its decor subtle with many shades of iridescent cerulean blue. In the centre of the room stood a old-fashioned brass-railed bed; in it lay Pandora – eyes closed and apparently sleeping

79

– her fine body clad in ivory silk, blatantly sensual in its attitude of repose. The blue pillow was swathed in the luxuriant fall of her brindled red-gold hair, and her pale face was relaxed and softly smiling. To be fair to her, he pictured in the slight irregularity of her leg, and some scars clearly visible through the silk. In a moment of seriousness, he examined his reactions – and found only tenderness and a strong urge to nurture. That, and an overwhelming need to see what else lay beneath that thin gown. The hot sexy thing that was covered – for the moment – in delicate pure silk-satin and beneath that, graced with the soft living fur of her sex. Jake could see the faint dark shadow of it, mysterious beneath the fabric that gleamed across her loins.

She was sleeping, yes, but she was waiting for him. A magnum of Champagne stood in a cooler by the bed, and alongside it were two fine crystal goblets. A mound of caviare lay temptingly over cracked ice, its tiny black globules looked fat and sexy. Soured cream and crackers were arranged close by. Oysters were unnecessary, Jake decided. He was already aching with lust.

In his solitary shower, he tried to conjure the tangy salt roe on to his tongue, the fizzing Champagne, the tart richness of the cream. Then, in an imagination within that imagination, he strove for the flavour of Pandora's sex.

In his mind's eye, the dream-dreamer stirred and the silk tightened across her intoxicating form. Moaning, Jake worked up a thick lather and took his prick in his foam-covered hand. In reality she wasn't here to make things happen, so he'd have to to do the business for himself . . .

Slowly, so slowly, he moved his fingers over his trembling erection. There was plenty of time; he mustn't spoil it.

'Jake?' the apparition spoke and he went winging back to his dream. 'Jake, is that you?'

The strange, dark eyes fluttered open, and Pandora drew herself gracefully to a sitting position. Jake's flesh leapt as the silky nightdress, caught beneath her body, slid down and exposed one full, milk-white breast.

'Oops!' she exclaimed, placing one long hand artfully over the bared globe. Her lacquered red nails looked stunning against the pure white skin beneath. Minx that she was, she let her rosy, puckered nipple peep between her first and middle fingers, and in a blatant gesture she tweaked her own body, drawing out the teat as if she were offering it to Jake's lips.

Which, as controller of this little fantasy, Jake decided she was! Within the fantasy, he strode forward, his whole attention fixed on that nub of pink flesh. Well, perhaps not all his attention. He had a little to spare for nipple's gorgeous twin, so clearly visible beneath the thin satin that covered it.

'Pandora,' he murmured, leaning over to fasten his lips around the exposed jewel, while his fingers found its silk-covered mate.

She was hard with desire for him, the tiny crests protruding insolently into his mouth and fingers. He sucked – and pinched – and she moaned incoherently, wafting her slim, lightly-clothed body against him. Immediately, the dreaming Jake dressed himself in a robe as insignificant as her nightdress. If romance was the keynote, a little mystery on his side wouldn't go amiss either.

Bemused, he leaned back against the shower wall, distancing himself from the fantasy for a moment although continuing to stroke his cock.

'Hang on a minute, Mallinson,' he instructed, laughing out loud at himself. 'Who the bloody hell's fantasy is this anyway' I ought to spread her and fuck her, and be done with it! What's all this pussyfooting around in aid of? She isn't even here!' Yet, irresistibly, he had to believe she was.

'Get with it, Jake,' he told himself, taking a firm hold on both his prick and his mind. 'At least this way, I get Pandora. If I'm going to get her, I might as well make it as nice for her as it is for me.' Locking all the sensual seduction paraphernalia firmly back into place, he set his internal camera rolling.

Body, silk, silk, body; the sandwich was certainly arousing enough for now, especially while he was nibbling Pandora's nipple and getting a succession of gutteral moans and involuntary writhings for his efforts. Oh God, if this was what she was like when he sucked her breast, what would she be like when he went down on her? The temptation to splice straight to *that* sequence was almost painful.

But he resisted. There was plenty of time. He wanted this to last and, inexplicable as it seemed to his insistent prick, he wanted the non-existent Pandora to enjoy herself too. One last pull on her delicate breast-tip, and he released her, then moved up to place a kiss on her cheek, 'I'm getting too excited, honey,' he whispered out loud. 'Shall we have a glass of Champagne to cool off? I don't want to come too soon, Pandora. I want this to be really special for you. I want to give you a hundred orgasms before I even have one.'

'You're an ambitious man, Jake Mallinson,' she murmured with a smile, 'but please feel free to try!' Pulling back, Jake admired the perfect shape of her breast as it glistened under its coating of saliva. The sheen accentuated the magnificence of the proud high curve, and made the swollen nipple look unbearably lewd.

That's it! thought Jake in his shower, enjoying the water cascading down his body. I'll drink Champagne from her breasts! And maybe . . .

Assessing the seductive banquet, he imagined the oceanic flavour of caviare combined with the taste of Pandora herself – the rich lusciousness of cream blending delicately with her smoky juice. Dropping his prick, he toyed for a second with spinning the shower dial to cold. It was all too vivid; his flesh was twitching madly, he'd erupt any second if he didn't hold back.

Back in his fantasy, he poured a brimming flute of Champagne and offered it to Pandora's Russian Red mouth; then watched the sexy undulation of her throat as she swallowed the sparkling wine with unashamed relish. God, everything about her drove him wild!

Topping up the glass he offered her more, and when she'd drunk her fill, he took a few sips from the selfsame glass. Setting it aside he prepared her a caviare-loaded cracker, then topped it with a little cream.

'Mmmm,' she murmured suggestively as she swallowed the titbit.

'More?' he enquired, poundingly aroused again.

'Yes, please!' purred Pandora, and Jake complied, his cock pulsing as he daubed on far too much cream and it seemed about to fall on the sky-blue sheet. Like a flash, Pandora caught the overflow and took it to her lips, pushing three fingers into her mouth and sucking them obscenely.

'You're a filthy woman, Pandora Jackson!' he growled, dragging her hand from her mouth and feeding her the second richly-topped cracker.

Again, she swallowed it in the rudest way imaginable, then licked the slick of cream from her perfect cupid's bow lips in a long, sensuous double swipe of her tongue.

'And you're a damn fool, Jake Mallinson,' he told himself back in the real world. 'You'll hit the tiles with your come any second if you go on like this.' Before he could think twice and stop himself, he flicked the thermostat to blue – then yelped and yowled as the icy water pummelled his erection into submission. He let the cold water stream over him for a minute, then brought the flow-heat back to 'moderate'. Looking down, he saw his cock was flaccid again. 'Okay then, super-tool,' he told it, 'let's start again, shall we?'

'Aren't you having anything to eat?' enquired Pandora when he returned to her. She was lolling back against the pillow again now, her body succulent and her pose inviting. Jake was glad he'd designed her gown a shade too tight.

'I'm saving my appetite,' he replied, his gaze fixed on the shaded delta of her near-visible pubic curls.

'Aren't you even the tiniest bit hungry?' she teased.

'I'm bloody ravenous, you saucy whore!' he told her as his erection resurfaced after its dowsing – and in the sybaritic fantasy, he closed in on their banquet. His mind was full of outrageous ideas; naughty schemes to employ the various ingredients. The only trouble was . . . Pandora wriggled so much when he played with her that food and fine wine would end up all over the place. He'd better find a way to curb her wigglings, delicious as they were, and make sure that everything he applied to her slim white body went exactly where he wanted it to!

Instantly, his imagination produced the answer –

a dressing-table drawer half-open, and hanging from it a number of long silk scarves. He checked out the brass head and footrails of the luxurious bed; it was conveniently just the right size.

'You're a feast, Pandora,' he murmured, worrying her neck with a few exploratory nibbles while his eager hands enclosed her silk-covered breasts. Cupping and lifting, he kneaded them in a distinct circular motion, and Pandora made a low, feline sound in her throat. She liked her romance a little on the rough side, did the good designer, and Jake was more than happy to oblige her. He squeezed the heavy orbs, as if testing for ripeness, and her bottom moved rythmically against the mattress.

'Yes, lady, you're a feast,' he repeated, 'juicy . . . soft and tender. I'm going to devour every scrap of you!' he nipped at the upper slope of one breast and she whimpered. 'But first you need trussing!'

'Jake! What're you doing?' she demanded, a thin streak of panic in her soft harmonious voice.

'Just whatever I want! And you're not going to stop me, lady! Now stretch your arms back across the pillows, and spread your legs. Wide!'

Enjoying his own chauvinism, yet knowing in real life he probably wouldn't get away with it, Jake slid down the tiles to sit – his own legs outstretched – in the shallow water of the shower trough. It was going to be a zonker of a climax when it came; he'd be a fool to be standing when he lost control of his limbs!

He closed his eyelids against the light, warm stream and saw Pandora behind them, spread-eagled and ready to be tied.

The scarves, of course, were precisely the right length. It was a simple matter to secure her and he lavished her bad leg with special and caring attention. Caressing it gently as he positioned it, he bent over her ankle, her calf and her knee in turn, to lay his mouth against each long pink scar. There was no fear in her eyes as he did so.

'What now?' she asked huskily, licking her lips again as if she knew how much it excited him.

'I'm going to taste you, Pandora,' he said bluntly, moving to sit beside her, 'I'm going to get this pretty thing out of the way,' he ran his hand over the silk at her flank, 'and I'm going to eat you.'

'Do it then!' she taunted, flirting her crotch towards him, seemingly unhampered by either her bonds or her lameness.

'In my own time, sexy lady,' he said, trailing his hand lightly across her belly. 'A perfect meal should be savoured. Every mouthful appreciated to the utmost. So I'm going to consume you very slowly, Pandora. Inch by delicious inch . . .'

'Just so long as you get there eventually,' she murmured, feigning nonchalance although Jake could see a pulse beating furiously in her neck. Tempted, he pressed his lips to the throbbing place and sucked a small patch of skin into his mouth. He considered love-biting her, then decided not to. He'd save his lips and tongue for more succulent places. He pushed up the white silk skirt and bunched it roughly at her waist.

Just the sight of her was a banquet!

Pandora's thighs were long and slim – and even the damaged one was relatively unmarked. Her belly was smooth and softly rounded, and her sex exquisite, lush and mouthwatering. Her feminine hair was full and flossy, but not so dense that he couldn't see the sensual blood-filled lips it guarded, or the small delicate bud of flesh he'd soon be teasing. The temptation to place his hand at her crotch immediately was enormous.

But he didn't. It was to be a long, slow meal. Circumspection was especially necessary, Jake decided in the shower. His tool was rampant again only moments after its icy dowsing. In the fantasy, he threw off his imaginary robe, placed a single kiss on Pandora's trembling clitoris, then, ignoring her moans and entreaties, returned his attention to her breasts.

The elegant silk nightdress fastened down the front – as far as the waist – with a set of tiny ribbon bows. Jake undid these slowly and meticulously, but left the satin draped across Pandora's heaving curves until the very last second. Only then, and with a good deal of flourish, did he bare her.

Her nipples were like small, pink stones crying out to be fingered.

'Beautiful breasts,' he murmured, praising the sight he'd never truly seen. 'I'm going to bathe them in Champagne.'

'Don't you d—' Pandora yelled, then squealed as half a flute of chilled fizz was trickled over the entire surface of her chest.

The Champagne went everywhere – soaking the sheets and the silk gown as well as the sumptuous body it was aimed at. But enough remained on the twin targets to leave them moist and glistening, and a siren call to Jake's ravenous mouth. Leaning naked across her, he made his tongue flat and broad and spread the vintage wine all over her nipples and areolae, then continued over the full beautiful sweep of each engorged breast. He washed her creamy skin with Champagne, and every long stroke made her purr with pleasure.

'I'm all sticky,' she complained, not really complaining at all.

'You sure are!' said Jake, his fingers inside her at last. Pandora strained at her bonds, her pelvis rising to him as he dabbed gently at her clitoris, his mouth still glued to one breast.

She was already wet: deliciously slippery and perfectly primed for a long smooth ride. There was nothing to stop him sliding straight in her to the hilt.

But that wasn't the way Jake wanted it to be. They'd strayed from the 'romance' remit somewhat, but as Pandora was so vociferously pleased with the situation, it didn't seem to matter.

We're running something of mine now, thought Jake ruefully, pulling slowly on his rod as the water flowed around his submerged backside. The warm rippling sensation was like a subtle caress and he wriggled in the warm, barmy swirl and watched his prick jerk accordingly.

Yeah, we're running something of mine, he observed again. But God knows what! His phantom fingers flickered Pandora's sex, noted the oiled silk texture of her juices, and seeded the craziest idea. He eyed the Champagne again, then the caviare, and finally the cream.

'What on earth are you up to?' whispered Pandora huskily, her body moving involuntarily under his gentle fondling. 'For God's sake bring me off, you tease! Look, Jake, either suck me or screw me, but whatever you do, do it now!'

'Such impatience,' he taunted, aping Pandora's soft, humour-the-client-he's-paying-a-fortune tones, but secretly thrilled by her earthy demands.

'Jake!'

'Okay, lady. Just you lie still there. I want to try something.'

Amazingly, she obeyed him, but it seemed to cost her some effort. He watched for a moment as she bit her velvety lower lip and scrunched her eyes tight shut. In no way a cruel man, Jake decided it was time to stop the teasing.

Holding open her pillowy blood-filled labia, he took a heaped spoonful of the soured cream and dropped it – in a single dollop – directly on to her clitoris. It oozed slowly down over the fruit-red tissues of her sex, clinging and shimmering deliciously. He added more and more until her whole vee was covered and he could see it bubbling in the pulsing mouth of her vagina.

'You dirty beast,' she chuckled, opening her eyes to see his trick – although Jake suspected she'd already sussed exactly what he was up to. 'I hope you're going to lick that off!'

'Try and stop me, lady. Just try and stop me . . .!' Within seconds he was crouched between her wide-open legs and perusing the lovely cream-coated sex in between.

Hmm . . . The idea of taking her seized him. Reaching over and supporting Pandora's head for a couple of seconds, he first kissed her on the mouth, then slid the satin pillow from behind her neck and repositioned it under her bottom. She bounced and whimpered when he took the opportunity, while he was in the vicinity, to finger the tender rose of her arsehole and slither some cream down deep along the groove.

'Don't . . . Oh God . . . Yes!' she babbled, 'For Christ's sake, get on with it!'

She was perfect now; perfectly positioned, perfectly ready. He dabbed on another spoonful of cream; then, grinning his wickedest grin, he flung the spoon away and tipped the whole dishfull straight on to her crotch. She moaned as he massaged it into the pretty reddish curls, her cries getting louder.

He murmured his response, playfully teasing her slippery labia. 'Irresistible!'

With that he placed his face between her legs in search of nectar and ambrosia. His goal arched towards him, a heavenly cup offered to his hungering mouth as Pandora's slim hips hovered inches above the blue satin. The tastes and the textures were so sublime that Jake devoured the contents of her sex, and while tongueing her, mixing the cream with her musky and abundant juices. Pandora mewled as he gently lapped and by the time he'd blended the cocktail to his liking, she was screaming; her frantic voice ringing out in extreme and tormented ecstasy.

Using his curled tongue, Jake scooped up a great swirl of cream-thickened juice and anointed her clitoris with it. Then, with a murmur of 'beautiful, beautiful, beautiful', he enclosed the tiny organ in his lips and sucked as if it were the source of life itself. Pandora's body arched like a bow, went rigid, and, as Jake pressed his whole face into her sex, he felt her vagina pulsating wildly against his chin.

'I'm coming! I'm coming! I'm coming!' she keened in a long, rising wail – and as she did, Jake's own loins were consumed by the same fabulous fire.

'So am I!' he sobbed in wonder, as his vision of cream and flesh and silk dissolved and he watched his semen – his own cream – trickle slowly down the tiles and merge with the burbling swirl below.

'Bon appetit, Pandora,' he murmured. Resting his head back against the shower wall, he dozed off as the water beat relentlessly down on his slack, sated body.

It was the phone that pulled him from his sudden slumber. Leaping clear of the still teaming shower, he dragged a towel round his hips, ran, and grabbed up the receiver just in time.

'I thought you weren't going to answer,' accused Pandora, her slightly flummoxed tone making Jake wonder if she hadn't wanted him to.

'I was in the shower . . . But it's okay. How can I help you?'

'I . . . I've . . . I've been thinking about what you said about the commission . . . and . . . er . . . *us*. I wondered if you'd like to come over to my place for dinner? It's only a scratch meal, but . . . Well . . . I really think we should talk.'

'Great! Wonderful! I'd love to!' Jake couldn't tell which was thudding the hardest: his heart or the blood in his reborn erection. 'What's on the menu?'

'Nothing too fancy, I'm afraid,' came the soft strangely excited answer, 'I thought we'd start with crudités and sour cream dip. Does that sound okay?'

'Oh, yes,' murmured Jake, his eyes closing in ecstatic expectation, 'Oh God, yes it does!'

Thirty-Six Hours

THIRTY-SIX HOURS. It was all we had. I didn't know how to tell him . . .

I could see him beyond the barrier, his face alight with smiles. How could I kill that joy by telling him how soon I'd be gone again?

'Aura! Aura, baby, here!' I could hear him calling. See him angling his way forward from amongst the waiting throng. And for perhaps the thousandth time since we'd met, I wondered what I'd done to deserve such a prize.

Davy Hashimoto . . .

I could feel my strong, soldier-girl's knees go weak as he darted forward to meet me. My beautiful little Davy, my helpmeet, my lover . . . and my very best friend in the world.

'Oh, baby, it's so good to see you!' His arms were already around me as he spoke, and I was wrapped in his warmth and his fine, male scent. I could well imagine the envious look of my fellow female squadmates . . . Even some of them men would be jealous.

My lovely Davy the sculptor. How I'd longed to be with him again! I still couldn't figure out why I called him 'little'! He was five eleven in his socks – when he wore them – and strong and fit, if a touch on the skinny side. His body was sleek and powerful . . . as a man, he was more than substantial. Far more! I felt my own flesh twitch and moisten. Soon, McCarthy soon! Use a bit of that military training of yours, woman . . . Contain yourself!

'Hello, there, stud, how've you been?' I enquired, back in command as I pulled away. Well, a sort of command. I could feel that old familiar heat down below. The hot, dark need I always felt if Davy was anywhere near me.

Fine, honey.' His thick lashes flickered, shading those long brown eyes of his: mysterious, artistic, all-seeing eyes. Half-Japanese, and wholly and entirely beautiful. 'But I've missed you! I've missed you so much! Oh, my, do you look good!'

As an artist, he should've known better, but my beauty was in his beholding eye, I suppose, not mine. I was just an average-looking lady squaddie, not a dog, but not spectacular either. Davy was the one who looked stunning. And he'd made such an effort today, bless his heart! To welcome me home, he'd made a genuine, concerted effort to be tidy.

'Come on, hunk! Let's go home,' I murmured, conscious of how time was whizzing by, and how this man who did his best work in the raw – both as an artist *and* a lover – had managed to look so great in his clothes today, in my honour.

His shirt was baggy and a little crumpled but the soft, raw silk was pristinely, immaculately white. His jeans were old and faded ones, but freshly washed and patched. He'd even managed to find a halfway decent pair of sneakers to put on. At home he usually went barefoot . . . and bare anything else if he thought he could get away with it.

Temptation attacked in spades as we moved through the malls and walkways in the direction of our communal flat. After all these months, all I really wanted to do was touch him; fondle that perfect arse in those tight, pale jeans; take the soft little cotton tie out of his hair and push my fingers through the whole, thick, black-silk mass. I wanted to stroke his toffee-brown skin; caress him everywhere; kiss his eyes, his mouth, his belly and his superb young cock. I wanted to devour him, consume him, feast on his sexy beauty. Fill myself with his flesh, his come and his love . . . Fill myself so choc-a-bloc with him I could survive another ten months.

'So, what've you done? What've you sold?' I enquired as we entered the huge, long studio that made up most of our home. It was polite conversation time. We never jumped straight into bed, no matter how much we wanted each other. We'd been together a fair while but there was still a small sweet shyness between us, a freshness that kept things exciting.

I even blushed when we faced one of his finished sculptures together.

'Not this one,' he said quietly.

I could see why. It was me. My body portrayed faithfully by hands that knew it so well. My face suggested and embeautied by hands that moved with equal skill over both clay and my own human flesh.

'You've flattered me . . .'

'No . . . Not at all, love. Clay doesn't lie.' He smiled, and I saw his long fingers flexing. Was it me he wanted to smooth them over? Or was it the simulacrum . . . the sculpture? I felt nervous; wanting but ridiculously scared. My whole body was aching now. My panties were wet. Yet I still wanted it to be Davy who asked; Davy who started it; Davy who led me to our bed.

I suppose it was to prove my femininity. I wanted to take orders, not give them; respond, not initiate. Here with him, I was just Aura – not the high-flying super-efficient Squad Sergeant McCarthy.

'What's in the fridge then?' I asked, changing the subject, shying away from decision. 'What've we got to eat and drink?' I walked through to the kitchen nook, intensely aware of Davy just behind me: silent, light-footed and lithe.

'I made some stew,' he began, biting his lip when I turned around in horror. 'I thought we could just heat it up . . .'

I groaned. I hardly dare open the refrigerator. There was just one manual skill that Davy had never mastered – cookery.

There was something hideous in a casserole on the second shelf. It probably *could* be heated up, but it certainly couldn't be eaten!

'Oh, Davy!'

'Yeah, I know . . . It's gruesome! Shall we go out for a pizza?' That questioning note in his voice, and the sweet boyish smile that went with it, just melted my heart. I could eat *him*, never mind his dreadful stew!

Suddenly I felt hot and shaky, unbearably excited. I thought about what I'd just thought . . . and I knew I'd never felt hungrier. To find a scrap of control, I reached into the fridge and took out a bottle of Astrapure. My lips were parched but they needed to be soft and moist and pliant. I popped the cap and glugged some of the fizzy water straight from its plastic bottle. I couldn't stall any more; I took another long drink, then put the water aside.

Turning to Davy, I wiped my mouth. I was still starving, and he'd never looked more appetising.

'Yes. We can go out, if you like . . .' Of its own volition, my hand floated out and settled on the crotch of his jeans, 'Or I could have a little snack first . . . It's up to you.' Please, Davy, I begged silently. Make *this* decision for me. Read my mind.

'Oh, yes, baby, yes!' he crooned, throwing back his head and closing his eyes as I squeezed him. 'Oh, yes, my love . . . my love, my love, my love . . .' His full crotch bumped into my grip, flaunted foward . . . and my decision was made for me – wonderfully.

A supplicant in khaki, I fell to my knees as Davy slumped back against the fridge door and spread his long lean legs to brace them.

'Do it, Aura! Do it!'

Euphoric, I leapt to obey. I flipped open his belt buckle, then unfastened his button-front jeans. Beneath the denim, his red cotton jock was hugely tented and a patch of dark, spreading moisture said everything I wanted to know. I looked into his face – and his eyelashes fluttered. Soft and black and heavy they signalled 'Go on! Go on!'

My fingers shook as I slid down his underwear and eased out his shivering cock.

Oh God, how I'd missed him! Missed *this*! His beautiful flesh, so stiff and rosy, the fat tip bulging and glistening. Veins throbbing beneath the velvet shaft . . . Totally alive . . . Primally male . . . The body of the man I loved.

With a great surrendering sob, he pushed his hips forward. His prick touched my open lips and I took the velvet knob inside my mouth and laved it all wet with my tongue – loving his salty man-taste and his long, soft whimper of pleasure.

His strong sculptor's hands closed tightly round the back of my head, and I revelled in being forced to take more. His glans probed my throat ... His pubic fluff tickled my worshipping face ... The clean scent of lemon filled my head ... That, and something more ancient and insidious: the heavy musky smell of an aroused, sweating man. My man.

Holding him as deep as I could without choking, I flirted and probed and worked him. My tongue went wild and my hands slid around his beautiful arse to pull him in closer than ever.

'Oh God, baby, I've missed you,' moaned my sweet pumping echo – wagging his lean flat hips as my fingers found the seam of his jeans. He couldn't last long; I could almost hear his semen churning. It was ready to rise, and I wanted it! I wanted his taste and his ecstasy. The sound of his breaking voice as he screamed out aloud in his climax.

Come, baby, come! I urged him, the words ringing silent in my head as I darted and dove with my tongue.

With a great, great cry he answered and obeyed, filling my mouth with his creamy heat, and his slippery silkiness ... His smooth male liquor nourished my loving heart and fed the soul that adored him.

'Oh dear, now what've we done?' he said a few minutes later, as we lay cuddled together on the kitchen floor; arms around each other and backs against the refrigerator door as we studied the results of what I'd just done.

Uninhibited as ever, Davy flipped at his softened prick with one slender, elegant forefinger.'Not much use to you for a while yet, babe,' he observed, his dismay only feigned as he leaned inwards to kiss my neck, 'but not to worry, I've still got these—' He wiggled *all* his fingers in a way that made me quiver from head to foot. 'And this!' Like a demon impish boy he stuck out his wet pink tongue . . . and one particular part of me quivered far more than the rest.

'Maybe I should have a snack too,' he murmured, tugging at the belt of my fatigues . . .

'How long have we got, babe?' he asked at last. It was the question I supposed he'd been wanting to ask since I'd first appeared through the customs barrier; the one I least wanted to answer.

We were still lying on the floor, but in the studio den now, naked, snuggled in blankets and surrounded by the remnants of several large pizzas.

'Thirty-six hours.' I glanced up at the clock on the wall, and hated what I saw. 'Well, more like thirty now.'

'Oh God.' There was pain in his eyes, but then, being my sweet amenable Davy, he smiled.

'Do you think you can survive on my cooking tomorrow?' he asked, quirking his fine black brows as he shimmied free of his blanket. His body was so brown and strong, his cock so proud and rising. Suddenly, my own body felt very hot, very hampered, and much too covered up . . .

'There's always the pizza-on-wheels-man, honey.' I wiggled my way out of my woollen cocoon and edged closer to his naked male shape. 'But why?'

'Because, my love,' he said softly, reaching for me and letting his hands close gently on my breasts, 'with only thirty-six hours for this, we haven't got time to go out!'

Hand in Glove

ALL WORK AND no play makes Jack a very tired boy . . .

J.J. massaged after-bath rub into the muscles of his shoulders and chest, and sighed. Tension popped beneath his fingers; knots of it nagged at his arms and back. His whole body was a great mass of aches.

That's the last time I put so much into one lousy job, he told himself, stretching hard then letting go in a release so delicious he almost came. He rolled his head from side to side, shrugged, then grinned. Okay, so he always put all of himself into everything. But at least next time, Madam could come round herself and ask him nicely!

There was no point letting *her* wind him up again. Because, one: the job was done now; two: in his heart of hearts he was actually grateful to her – *very* grateful. She'd handed him the biggest break of his whole career. Finally, three: he didn't like admitting it, but in a strange screwed-up sort of way he really got off on her! He'd never experienced anything like

99

it before; he'd been aroused for the whole four weeks he'd worked on this job. Pushing his wet hair out of his eyes, he sighed again; a puzzled and worn-out man.

The night was hot, far too hot, so J.J. stayed naked. Wandering through into his lounge-come workroom, he studiously avoided both the sheaves of drawings strewn across every available surface and the glowing screen of his computer, and padded over to the sideboard to look with real happiness at his small but carefully chosen selection of bottles.

He never drank while he was designing – sobriety gave his work a keener edge – so this first drink afterwards was pure heaven. It always seemed doubly strong! After four interminable weeks slaving over Chantel Lindsey's darkly moody film sets, this one shot of icy single malt packed all the punch of every drink that J.J. had ever taken.

Up yours, Chantal! he toasted silently as the whisky slithered down his throat like velveteen fire. Next time, lady, have the grace to meet your drone in person!

The set he'd designed for her was good – an Oscar winner? – but even now, he still couldn't figure out why he'd worked himself to a standstill for a woman he'd never met.

Chantal Lindsey – the creative despot of her own red-hot production company – was demanding and brilliant, and absolutely specific in her written instructions. But she was never available in person. J.J. had always worked hand in glove with his producers before Ms Lindsey's non-presence, plus her stream of tersely pithy faxes and the imperious notes she'd scrawled on his early sketches, had really pissed him off!

Yet that same resentment had been the grit in a pearl; Madam Chantal had fired up his visionary juices and the outcome was the finest work he'd ever done.

Sipping his Hebridean nectar, J.J. reached back to knead his aching shoulder. God, that Chantal was such a ball-breaker!

What I need now, he observed sagely, is to give her a damn good grudge fuck! Especially as I've lived like a monk for the last month . . . Drink wasn't the only thing he'd had to give up.

Already partially aroused, J.J. set his mind to the possibility of sex; reviewing his possible bedmates as he topped up the level of his drink. Although unattached at present, he had several womanfriends he could ring and take out for the evening. Women who'd be more than happy to drink with him, eat with him, then, later, without question or embarrassment, let him take them to his bed.

It'd be a rip-off though. What the hell good was he to a woman right now? Self-absorbed and strung out, he'd nothing to give. Okay, so he could get an erection – he'd *already* got one! – but getting it up and keeping it up didn't automatically make the earth move.

Even so, he was still unbearably randy . . . and getting more so by the second. Damn you, Chantal Lindsey! he cursed the faceless woman. It's your bloody fault! I could die for a fuck, but I'm too screwed up to go and out and get one!

But he didn't have to go out and make like a superstud, did he? He'd got privacy, comfort, his own right hand . . . And, goddammit, he *was* supposed to be creative!

You're the designer, J.J. old son – design a fantasy! Design yourself some sex.

Settling carefully into his chair, he shimmied down so his buttocks were slightly spread. The leather seat felt exquisitely chilly against his bare behind, stark and sweet like the touch of a mystery woman. He used his mind to make the seat her hands, then wriggled deeper to make her caress him.

Taking a long pull of whisky, he swivelled the chair so he could put his glass aside. Re-adjusting his position, he pushed down, splitting himself a little more, and his cock reared up like a great red prong, raunchy and magnificent, right in the centre of his eyeline. Placing his hands palm-down on his lean brown thighs he teased his stiffened-flesh by denying the contact it ached for.

'You've got a beauty there, J.J.,' he murmured, clenching his groin and loving his own rod as it waved before him like a thick, lengthy reed.

She'll love it too, said a voice inside his head. A voice that was his own yet transformed by his need and a growing sense of excitement.

She? What 'she'? As his head grew light and his breathing laboured, he searched his mind for a partner: a cool goddess for his heated solitude. No face appeared, but suddenly it didn't matter; content with her anonymity, he took his shaft in his hands and began, slowly, to pump.

Deep in the luscious depths of the experience, everything was right on target; yes, even at this very first stage. J.J. had never had hang-ups about masturbation; he enjoyed it thoroughly and did it often. To him it was a celebration of his own sensuality that brought scope and richness to all other sex. He watched the long slide of his hand on his cock; the skin was still dry to the touch as yet, creating tantalising friction between fingers and shaft. Shaking slightly, he set his mindfilm running and drew upon the imagery of his recent designs. As his eyes closed, he waited for a woman to appear in his set . . .

He was alone in the middle of his own creation, the dark monochrome alley that still flickered on his computer screen. It was somewhere on the outskirts of a sprawling futuristic city, and deserted. Twilight gleamed greyly, and the faint thud-thud of hard rock music told him he was near an entertainment area. He felt excellent now: strong and sexy, ready for anything, and deep deep into his fantasy.

'Hello, J.J.'

A woman's voice: commanding but not strident, powerful yet soft as silk. In the dream, he froze in his tracks; in reality his cock leapt and he gripped it just under the crown to tame its volcanic arousal. He mustn't come yet. There was still a long long night ahead . . .

'Stop right there,' said the unseen woman. She was in shadow, but J.J. could make out a tall, slim, dark-clad form. 'Stand against the wall. Completely still. Put your hands behind your head.' Because it was a dream, he obeyed without question, and the woman moved partially into view.

His fantasy was skilfully lit. He could see a slender neatly-curved body a grey leather suit . . . but no face. 'Mystery Woman' wore a sleek, *haute couture* garment that was as fine and tasteful as she was. This was class he was dealing with: hard, chic class. An indefinable resonance told him he ought to know her, though there was still no recognition. Her features remained frustratingly in shadow, veiled in a grey far darker than that of her suit. Only her voice defined her as beautiful . . .

'Well, what have we here?' Her drawl made the

hairs on the back of his neck stand up one by one and his prick throb slowly and painfully. The very words seemed to dance along the whole pulsing length of him . . .

She was standing in front of him now, her face still obscured, and he jumped in both body and penis when she pressed her leather-gloved hand to his groin. He groaned long and low as she squeezed him.

'Silence!'

The single quietly-spoken word synchronised perfectly with her left-handed slap across his face. The pressure on his cock and balls stayed precisely the same, his sex delicately vised between her grey-clad fingers. In reality, J.J.'s hand fell away as his prick quivered ominously.

'You will not speak in my presence,' she went on as she released his genitals, her tone honeyed and deceptively conversational. In the dream *she* had every right to command, and had J.J. no option but to obey. 'Press your back to the wall. Spread your legs slightly. Lift your buttocks. Bring your crotch towards me.'

Simple commands. Short, to the point, no compromise. In the dream, J.J. complied without question; back in the reality of his room, he shuffled his naked bottom deeper into the leather-covered chair, dilating his anus to kiss the smooth cold hide. Why is it, he wondered as his cock swayed and trembled, why is it I get off on her ordering me around? Why the hell do I love it so much?

In both worlds his thighs twitched . . .

'You may take your hands from behind your head,' she said pleasantly. Dream-time J.J. let his arms flop, his hands hung loosely by his denim-clad haunches. 'Now . . .' He could hear her smiling.

104

'Unzip your flies, push down your underpants, and expose your prick and balls.'

'Lady—'

Smack! His face flamed again.

'Shut the fuck up and do it!'

Still the same satin-soft voice, and in his imagination he hurried to do its bidding. In both worlds his eyes watered from the slap, but in the here and now he laid a hand carefully on his prick again. Testing. Assessing. As he squeezed cautiously a drop of juice swelled at the tip and, working with the slow craft of a surgeon, he spread the fluid down his shaft and began – with equal precision – to work the moist surface skin over the hard inner core.

Still dry though . . .

Reaching for his drink, he took a long sip, swirled the smoky fluid in his mouth then swallowed. Releasing his tool, he put the fingers that'd held it into his mouth. His own slight saltiness lingered a second then submerged into the taste of the Scotch. Sucking hard, he coated all four fingers in whiskified saliva and took them, glistening to his cock. The trace of spirit made his taut flesh sting and J.J. rolled his hips, savouring the sensation as his mind reeled out the fantasy.

The teeth of his imaginary zip bit nastily into his balls; his jeans were too tight to expose him comfortably and his tender, swollen testicles were forced up against the root of his prick. He was mortifyingly rigid and the woman's hidden eyes homed in like lasers. Then, as if dream-thought summoned dream-reality, a bright narrowly focused light was shining directly on his tense, shivering organ.

'A beauty,' she murmured.

That's what I thought, echoed real J.J., gingerly stroking the real flesh.

'Rub it, J.J.'

'But—'

'Do it, J.J. Wank yourself or I'll hurt you again. Down there. Now do it!'

Rock and roll, my queen! thought J.J. as real and imaginary hands fused and launched into furious movement.

There was no time for exactitude now. Hugely turned-on, he pumped himself like a madman, wrenching the skin back and forth over the solid rod within.

'Holy shit!' he hissed, his teeth locked in a death-like rictus as he leather-clad fingers reached out, laced with his, and rode the length of his tortured, blood-filled pole. Fire tore down his spine then shot out of his prick as semen; he watched – from a million miles away – as fine stings of it arced high in the air, then hit the woman's dark skirt and trickled slowly towards its hem.

'Rock and roll, rock and roll . . .' he whispered again, thrilling to the tremors that rippled through his belly and thighs, and the feel of his now ultra-sensitive prick contained within their joined hands.

When his eyes fluttered open, he looked dazedly around. Where was she? His grey woman with her gloved hands and her slim, spunk-splattered skirt?

But there was no sign of his goddess. The room was unchanged. Except for . . .

'Oh, my God!' he said softly as he espied the computer monitor. Filaments of come were rolling down it, pale against the shades of grey, their whiteness warm on the cool dark background of Chantal Lindsey's deserted alley.

106

Six months later

It was so like his design it was frightening! Even the lighting was just as he'd imagined.

'She's around here somewhere,' the young PA had said, then scuttled away, as if she were as spooked as J.J. was by this shadowy, menacing alley.

Where was she, this hellcat who'd domineered him into creating this, and done it without one single instant of personal contact? Where was she, this Chantal Lindsey? And why, in this familiar alley, was he looking for someone else?

Suddenly he shuddered in delicious disbelief. Christ, he was erect! Any minute now there'd be a spotlight.

'Hello, J.J. . . .'

So soft and husky. Déjà vu grabbed him by the heart, throat and balls. It couldn't be! *She* couldn't be! It'd been a drunken vision. A wanker's mindgame!

Yet the voice spoke again . . . and was real. 'This all makes me feel as if I know you.' There was a faint movement in the shadows, a gesture that seemed to encompass the whole of their surroundings.

Then, to J.J.'s horrified joy, the discreet figure stepped forward, stealing his sanity with a chic dark suit with the soft gloss of leather and a pair of long, slim, immaculately begloved hands.

He hardly dared look at her face . . . but he did.

She wasn't particularly beautiful. Her even features, framed in a sleek cap of dark hair, were unremarkable apart from a pair of large, luminous light-dark eyes that glittered coolly in the gloom.

But it was her hands that held him hopelessly bedazzled. His stiffness magnified to a state of real

107

pain; he wanted to fall forward, double over himself, clasp his aroused agony in his *own* shaking hands.

She was reaching out now; a greeting, presumably, as she moved towards him. 'Congratulations, J.J., this's exactly what I wanted.'

This? The set or the meeting? She looked down thoughtfully at her fingers as if knowing what they'd done.

Please! Yes! No! Pleading silently, J.J. followed her glance.

If that hand touched him, that hand in its thin leather glove. If it ever touched him he'd come. And she'd know.

Trembling, aching, wanting, he lifted his arm, extended his fingers and . . .

Sweet Saint Nick

TALK ABOUT GETTING an eyeful!

Lying in a Casualty Department, wearing an eye patch, a party frock and a cloud of Shalimar wasn't quite what I'd expected of a 'girl's night out', but as it was supposed to be the season of good cheer and all that, I was trying to look on the bright side.

Mainly because there *was* one . . .

Closing my eyes – the good one and the one still stinging madly – I conjured up the last thing I'd seen with 20/20 vision.

Father Christmas's willie!

Well, not exactly the equipment of Old Saint Nick himself, but the large and rather beautiful tool of 'Big Saint Nick – The Lady's Christmas Cracker' who'd bared his all for us with a good deal of groin-thrusting flourish, and given me a smack in the eye with his G-string too!

God, it'd hurt! Like hell! But even so, I couldn't forget the view . . .

I'd been rather dubious about a male stripper outing, seeing as I was currently off men, but when Big Saint Nick had prowled on to the stage, I'd changed my mind pretty fast, then said a great big thanks to Janie for getting us a front-row table!

Technically, he'd kicked off his act in a Santa suit, but the beard, hood and skimpy red tunic were soon history, and he was treating us to far more than the average Christmas Cracker: a pelvis packed with power, swirling and thrusting like a tribal warrior's. His G-string was red velvet, minute but bulging, and had a fluffy white pom-pom bobbing and bouncing right where the action was!

It was all very tacky, but endearing somehow; personally, I couldn't imagine getting a better Christmas box than his!

Not that the rest of him wasn't just my type. Long black hair tied in a pony-tail, and a muscular, golden, but not too massive body that moved as if classically trained to dance. A nice face too: dark, naughty eyes, and an even naughtier mouth. One that seemed to be smiling specifically for me. It could've been wishful thinking, but it was *our* table he chosen for his *coup de grâce*.

And why, still starkers, had he leapt so quickly to the aid of the woman his scanties had wounded? Janie and Sally and Louise had fussed and panicked while he'd gone and got dressed; but it was he, not them, who'd brought me to the hospital and it was his soft white handkerchief I'd clutched to my tear-stained face all the way.

His name, funnily enough, really was Nick; and as the injury to my eye was quite minor and would have no lasting effects, I was secretly quite happy he'd twanged me. If he'd stay a while longer I'd be even happier!

'Carrie? Your friend's here to see you,' said the nurse who'd treated me. When I'd blinked and focused, the man at her side still looked good to me, even through only one eye!

110

'How're you feeling?' he asked, a delicious combination of contrition and machismo in one spectacular package.

'Oh, not so bad . . .'

No, not bad at all, seeing that face, and thinking of the even better body that went with it. 'There's no permanent damage. It hurts a bit, and I'll have to wear a patch for a day or two and use some drops, but otherwise I'll be absolutely fine.'

'Look,' he said, then grinned sheepishly because 'looking' was a sore point for me, 'I feel responsible. I want to be sure you're okay. The doctor said they'd given you something for the pain and it'd make you woozy. The least I can do is drive you home.'

"S all right. Don't go to any trouble,' I said, not meaning it. I *was* starting to feel spaced out. Sort of floaty and floppy and in need of a body to cuddle. There was no-one at home since Harry'd left, so why not accept? Season of goodwill and all that. It was time *I* had some goodwill. And he *was* gorgeous. *All* of him . . . It was easy to remember what was under that lambswool sweater, and more especially under those tight blue 501s!

In that fleeting moment, it'd been the nicest cock I'd ever seen: dark and hefty; thick and swingy and perky. Concentration was tricky at the moment, but it seemed to me he'd been rather perkier than he should've been given the laws on public decency and all that Mary Whitehouse-type stuff!

The thought of him getting a hard-on – right there on the stage, and for me – made me giggle insanely.

'Are you sure you're okay?' His handsome face creased in a worried frown. There was a thin film of oil still gleaming on his cheekbones and I thought of how it'd shone on his chest and his thighs . . . Oh God, even his cock had been oiled!

'Carrie! Are you all right?' he persisted.

I was well out-of-it. I'd only seen his tool for a split-second, but in my imagination it reared up and pointed in my direction; thick-veined and throbbing, oil glistening along its chunky length and glinting on its swollen, circumcised head.

'I'm fine.'

Lord, that stuff they'd shot me was strong! In my mind's unhampered eye, Nick was crouched over me, nude, erect and godlike, and just about to drive in right between my thighs. I could see him sliding, feel him moving, and my body went loose and wet.

I shook my head wildly to clear it, then spat out a foul word at the intense jolt of pain *that* caused.

'You're not fine at all, are you?' His hand was holding mine now, and his voice was firm, kind and utterly meltingly sexy! 'I don't want to hear any more about it. As soon as the doc gives the word, I'm going to drive you home and take care of you!'

'Okay, Santa . . . You win!'

I didn't try to shake off 'woozy' this time. I was all in favour of woozy if it kept my sweet Saint Nick at my side and gave me such outrageously detailed visions! My eyelids – both covered and uncovered – fluttered down, and behind them Nick was dancing again. In my bedroom, stark naked, heavily oiled and rampant, he moved far more explicitly than he'd done for his public audience. His long tanned hands traced his long tanned thighs, then he cupped his sex and pulled and squeezed and wanked and offered the whole thick clublike mass of it to me.

'Oh, yes . . .' Wanting, my free hand rose up and reached out. Then it was taken determinedly in his.

'You rest here,' he said as I blinked in disappointment at his fully-clothed body. He was frowning again and looking at me with a sharp, narrow-eyed expression that made me wonder if he'd sussed my craziness.

'Rest here.' He squeezed my hands. 'As soon as I get the go-ahead, I'll take you home.'

'Mmmm . . .' I was drifting again, the images not purely sexual this time, but cuddly and comforting too. My eye twinged briefly but then decided to settle.

I waited. I rested.

This is mad! I thought later, slumped dreamily in the passenger seat of his car as we sped towards my flat. I don't know this man from Adam. I've barely spoken half a dozen words to him. I've seen his cock, but I've no idea what's inside his head. He could be a psycho or a rapist!

Yet the cautious, conscientious medical staff had seen fit to entrust me to him. Who was I to argue? It was Christmas: season of good cheer. After the hassle I'd been through with Harry, it was about time I had some of that peace on earth, wasn't it? Or a piece of something! I giggled again, and Nick's eyes flicked briefly towards me, checked, then returned to their scrutiny of the road.

I seemed to spend the whole journey in a haze of sexy smells. My own Shalimar was still much in evidence, and so was the classic and pervasive man's cologne that drifted from the folds of Nick's jacket, a thick biker-style leather he'd draped round my shoulders to keep out the cold. It was Christmassy smell, Old Spice or something, and invigoratingly light and clean. But its freshness didn't affect me as much as some of the other odours floating around: darker scents; downer and dirtier; manssweat and musk, and the shocking, tangible aroma of my own female arousal.

I couldn't believe what was happening or how I was feeling. He'd nearly blinded me, and now I was lolling around in his car like an easy pick-up, speeding towards my flat where I'd surely ask him inside. Even so, I knew in my soul there was no real danger in Nick. He'd hurt me once, but he wouldn't hurt me again. I didn't just feel that, I *knew* it.

When we arrived, I discovered my body wasn't functioning as well as my mind. My legs buckled as I tried to unlock the door, and within seconds I was in Nick's arms and being Jane to his Tarzan as he carried me through my flat to the bedroom.

What followed would've been either mortifyingly embarrassing or sensationally erotic if I'd been firing on all cylinders . . .

Beautiful Nick undressed me – beautifully. He cleaned off my make-up – working like a surgeon around my battered eye – then washed me and bundled me into a nightgown. He performed the most intimate of services with gentleness and not the slightest lapse in propriety. He even helped me brush my teeth!

When he finally deposited me in my bed and tucked the duvet up round my ears, I was feeling decidedly peculiar, but in a decidedly wonderful way: pampered cossetted and charged with a light sexual fever. Nick's touch had been perfectly neutral, but my body wasn't! I was turned on, but not so intensely it made me uncomfortable. I was floating, my sex felt warm and moist, ready for love but deliciously relaxed. I put my arms up to pull Nick down beside me, then drooped and sighed and let myself be covered again. I felt as if I were outside myself and watching. Watching Nick brush my hair carefully back from my face, adjust the patch over my dodgy eye, then kiss me just once on the cheek.

'I'll stay here tonight just in case. My stuff's in the car. Is it okay if I use your shower? I'm still all yucked up with oil.'

'Mmmm . . . yeah . . . Shall I scrub your back?' Snuggled beneath the covers, I wondered vaguely if I'd actually got the energy.

'Look, you . . . sleep!' He laughed – a soft and incredibly sensual sound – and I must have obeyed because I never heard the water running.

My sleeping dreams weren't as straightforward as the ones I had awake. In the illogical dreamland world, I was sitting on the table in the nightclub with my skirt round my waist and my hand working furiously between my legs. *I* was the show, and the men on the stage were watching me! The sensation of exhibiting myself was supremely arousing and I was right on the point of coming when my ex-boyfriend Harry elbowed his way through the adoring throng, shouted 'Slut!' and punched me right in the eye! The pain felt like breaking glass and I crumpled into a ball like an injured child. Then suddenly Santa Claus was hugging me better and say, 'Hey, it's all right1 Take it easy!'

'Hey! It's all right! Take it easy!'

One minute I was thrashing around in my nightmare, the next I was cooing and sighing in a pleasant half-awake doze. A strong hand was stroking my shoulder.

Some fragments of the dream remained however. My own hand actually was between my legs, and I removed it as surreptitiously as I could. My eye was prickling slightly, but the sensation was less intrusive than the one running the length of my back – especially in the lower regions where my nightdress had rucked up to my waist. A solid column of heat was pressed close as close and I was being nestled gently against it; while a rather smaller but even more solid column was intent in burrowing itself into the crease between my thigh and the curve of my bottom!

'You were shouting in your sleep,' whispered Nick, still caressing my shoulder and showing no inclination to remove his cock from between my legs.

'I was having a funny dream.' Somehow, I just couldn't seem to help myself pushing back against his erection.

'Yes, I'd gathered that.' As his hand settled over mine, there was a smile in his voice and I blushed in the darkness, knowing that *he* knew precisely what *I'd* been so unconsciously doing.

We seemed locked in a kind of magic stasis – his hand on my hand on my belly, and his cock throbbing quietly away against my leg. It was like hovering on the brink of a huge and very tempting gulf – and wondering if you'd really got the guts to fly!

I suppose some things are inevitable, though. His hips bumped, I went 'Mmmm . . .' again and his hand left mine and started travelling.

One finger slipped slowly and silkily into my cleft, parted the hair, parted the soft puffy lips, then settled like light itself on my clit. The softest of pressures made me groan, and as Nick seemed to be in no hurry, we drifted into a long luxurious limbo time devoted purely to *my* pleasure.

Our bodies lay like spoons, I had his cock pressed snugly against my bottom and his hands at my breast and my crotch – stroking and palpating, delicately caressing and fingering. I suppose in the cold light of day, it could've seemed calculating and manipulative – push my buttons, turn me on – but in the special secret darkness it was a beautiful gift from a stranger. Whimpering and grabbing backwards at his thighs, I twined my feet around his and arched into my first sweet orgasm, my clitoris pulsing in long deep waves that raced on inwards from his steady, rubbing fingers.

He held me, gentled me, and made it happen and happen and happen again . . .

My 'Yes! Yes! Yes!' anticipated his simple uncomplicated questions.

'Are you ready? Do you want me?'

But when I moaned 'Yes!' again, he started to pull away.

'Look, Carrie, I'd better use something. I've some in my wallet . . .'

I couldn't bear not having him against me. 'No it's all right. Try the drawer behind you – in the bedside table.'

'You angel,' he whispered, kissing my neck, then turning away in the darkness. My back felt cool for a moment and there was a rustling, some small deft movements, and then his prick coming at me again, pressing strongly and encased in a condom. He teased it around my thighs, my labia and my moist slit, then took my hips in his big strong hands, tilted my pelvis and positioned himself carefully against my vagina.

'Guide me, love,' he purred in my ear.

It was a moment of perfectly balanced trust. I felt close to tears, loving his male vulnerability as I fed his warm length inside me.

Cradling me, cocooning me, curving his big dancer's body to warm my smaller, softer one, he slid one hand back between my thighs and pleasured my clit as he fucked me. His touch was so sure, so right, so even more beautiful than before

117

that I spasmed immediately around him.

Our movement was limited, but in paradise all motion is relative – I could fly and I *did*! On eddies of hot hard bliss, I rose and rose, buoyed up by my sweet strong Nick, my accidental man from nowhere, with his animal grace, his giving hands and his sturdy hard-driving prick.

It wasn't all one way, of course. Somewhere in my own ecstasies I heard him shout, and felt him convulse and grab and push, push, push as he came. He stretched me beautifully and shafted me deeply, and even in orgasm, he still rubbed and pressed and fondled so I could soar again with him.

Eventually I did get the sleep he'd intended for me, the deep, dreamless healing sleep that only good sex can give you.

I got the waking that goes with it too: a kiss, a gentle shake, and a steaming cup of perfectly perked coffee!

'You're still here,' I observed blearily, scrunching up my good eye as I put aside the cup and focused on Nick.

I woke up faster then. He was still naked, still gorgeous, and I – I realised now – just what I'd always wanted.

'Look, I know this is utterly crazy and you've probably got plans already . . .' I swallowed, wished I didn't look so stupid with my eye patch; wished I could just wake up in bed looking like Madonna or somebody. 'What're you doing for Christmas? Do you want to spend it here? We could make it nice and cosy. Get crackers and stuff . . . If you haven't got anything on, that is?'

For a moment his morning-stubbly face was perfectly expressionless . . . then he grinned, and

118

seemed to sparkle all over with pure sexy merriment. His hand dropped seductively to his lovely, beefy cock.

'Thanks, I accept.' He looked down at the large shaft thickening in his fingers. 'I don't seem to have anything at all on!' Very gently, he took my hand, then folded it around his erection in place of his own. 'But we can soon do something about that!'

Reaching into the drawer, he drew out another condom and smiled as he tore at the foil. 'Merry Christmas, Carrie. Let's start celebrating . . .'

Pretty Young Thing

I'D ALWAYS WANTED to sleep with him. Since the first moment I saw him: when he was just fifteen and I was living with someone else. I'd taken one look at that face and body – and in my mind we'd been naked and fucking.

It'd been impossible then, unthinkable: he was underage and the son of a schoolfriend I'd just re-discovered, and I was working hard at 'me and Peter', a relationship already on the skids without my looking elsewhere.

There'd been everything against Ross and me. All I could do was ogle and dream and blame stress and some kind of early mid-life crisis. But now – three years on – that 'everything' had changed.

I'd invited Joan to the villa for a spell, and though I could see she was dying to accept, she frowned suddenly, then started to dither.

'Can I bring Ross along too? He's really down in the dumps just now. Some little twit's jilted him and of course it's the end of the world. They take things so seriously at that age, don't they?'

I nodded, appalled at my own inner excitement on hearing his name.

It'd been a while since I'd last had sex – what with the bitterness over Peter – yet just that one word, that one short name, and my sex seemed warm, aching and empty.

I was annoyed too: cross with Joan. I was twice Ross Frazetti's age, yet *I* still took things seriously. It was easy for Joan to be dismissive; she'd dumped her unwanted Italian husband with an ease that made me shudder, and with precious little thanks for the beautiful son he'd given her.

It was late afternoon when they arrived. While Joan was happy to settle on the patio with a drink, Ross had disappeared off up to his room, lingering only long enough to make an even bigger impression on me than he had at fifteen. He was still the same pretty young thing he'd been then: a fine-boned, dark-haired poetic-looking boy. But now he was tall and had muscles too. Not to mention a raw, masculine grace, and a thought-provoking bulge in that most crucial of places!

It was more than simple, anatomical assets. This year's Ross had a hint of the big cat about him, a pure, yet discreet alpha-maleness as unstudied as it was exciting. But it was his eyes which really got to me: brown, almond-shaped and enormous, they held a pain that was heavy and dark and sexual. To me, those shadows were explicit; they said that for all his quietness and youth, Ross had loved – and fucked – and lost.

Despite that he wasn't a sulker; quite the reverse. Overturning his mother's pessimistic predictions, he came down promptly for dinner, and though it was obvious that *he* knew *we* knew he'd got problems, he smiled and chatted – and was gently and understatedly charming. I began to wonder what he was like when he was actually *happy*:

devastating, probably; unstoppable; fatal. I imagined myself having an orgasm right there at the table. But he ate next to nothing, and his handsome face was pale under its Mediterranean caramel glow, almost ghostly against the matte black cotton of his sombre shirt and jeans.

I couldn't eat either. Other hungers consumed me, and I drank to make them bearable. I felt a nice, sensual buzz building as I studied his long, slender-fingered hands; his soft, slightly pouting lower lip and those huge, hurting, sex-dark eyes. I wanted to take him in my arms and hug all his troubles away – then take his cock deep into my hungering body and finish the job completely!

And that, I suppose, was what woke me later. It was a shock to actually want someone again. The trauma of my break-up had numbed me. Even before that, out of sight and mind, Joan's black-haired son had been simply an exquisite, but occasional fantasy: something pretty to look at while I made myself come.

It was a hot night, but I pulled a thin shirt over my nakedness as I stepped out on to the veranda. Looking along, I saw that my guests, like me, had both left their French windows open for coolness.

The room next to mine contained Joan, snoring softly and sleeping the sleep of the pleasantly plastered. She'd matched my every glass of wine with a large hand-mixed Martini of her own, but never having had a hangover in her life, she'd probably just get a fantastic night's sleep and be ready to start again in the morning!

Barefoot, I judged my steps carefully as I approached the next window along. Then I stopped altogether. Vaguely familiar noises drifted from between the fluttering curtains.

Muffled sobs, small stifled groans; the sound of someone very young, male, and desperately, desperately unhappy. I hardly dared look into the room, but no power on earth could've stopped me.

He lay like a dark wraith in the middle of the wide white bed. His eyes were closed, his face contorted, and his right hand was wrapped tightly around his cock. Lost in grief, and wracked by unsatisfied desire, my sweet, sad Ross was wanking.

It was the most beautiful sight I'd ever seen, and the most arousing: moonlight, tears and an erection. The combination was intoxicating; my head felt light as thistledown and my sex grew wet and heavy.

I wanted that wide, rosy-tipped club inside me; that penis, that tool; the big, man's cock that sprang up from the loins of a gentle, troubled boy. I must've gasped or sighed or something, because Ross's eyes flew open, then went wide and blank with horror.

'No!' he cried indistinctly, 'Oh, no! Oh, no! Oh, no!' Before I could speak or move towards him, he'd abandoned his stiffened flesh and was dragging the sheets right up and over his blushing face and body.

'Ross! It's all right! Don't hide!' I called out softly.

'Please! Go away!' came a faint voice from beneath the white linen layers. 'Please go away, Mrs Lovingood! Please go. I'm sorry.'

'What's to be sorry for, Ross?' Trembling, I crossed the room and sat down on the side of the bed, 'The tears? Or the fact that you were touching yourself?' I'd seen it now. Seen what I most wanted. I had to stay and make him forget the girl who'd hurt him; or at least try to.

Slowly, feeling as if I were flushing out a scared forest creature, I teased the sheet down to his waist. His eyes glowed up at me from a face burning hot with embarrassment.

'I shouldn't have been—' He paused, snagging that soft lower lip between his teeth. 'I've no right to be doing *that* here in your house, Mrs Lovingood.' He turned away, his perfect profile cameoed by the whiteness of the pillow.

'My name's Amy.' I tugged the sheet clear of him, and his cock bounced up and slapped against his flat, gilded belly. 'And why shouldn't you masturbate here? I do.'

Ross seemed at a loss how to respond. His eyes flicked from his rampant body to my face, and his mouth dropped open in astonishment.

'Sex can heal as much as hurt, Ross,' I said quietly, edging closer. 'I've been lonely . . . Why shouldn't I give myself pleasure? Why shouldn't you give *yourself* pleasure? It can only make you feel better.'

His fingers curved slightly on the sheet, and his erection swayed. Something in him was reaching out to me – and I knew now that I could take what I wanted.

Ross. His body. His strong young cock.

'Let's help each other, sweetheart,' I whispered leaning over him and flipping open the buttons on my shirt. With a faint swish, it slid off my shoulders.

Ross's eyes widened even more, but I loved him for the knowing smile that formed on his lush young lips. He was shy; but not *that* shy. I'd surprised him, yes, but he wasn't a helpless virgin, or slow on the sexual uptake. Looking at the rigid bar of his prick, I felt my mouth water and my sex moisten. Foolish girl who'd rejected such a treat! His eyelashes fluttered like twin black fans and he arched his fabulous body towards me in an attitude of complete abandon.

You hussy! I accused him silently. You dirty little

flirt! In need and amusement I pressed my lips to his. How quick he was to adapt, to allure me. I ran my fingers down his flanks as he opened his mouth to my tongue and moaned around it, long and wantfully. His hips lifted as I kissed him, his hot flesh seeking a place to bury itself. In answer I lay full length upon him and massaged his tool with my belly. Two long flexible hands slid around my bottom and began – slowly – to knead.

I'd come with the half-formed idea of 'teaching' this boy something, but as he caressed the cheeks of my arse, and flicked his fingers delicately into my crack, I began to question my own assessment. He could well need some help with his relationships, but as the moments passed – and his hands grew bolder and his touch hotter – it was obvious he knew all he'd ever need to know about the erotic anatomy of women. Maybe that was it? He'd been *too much* for the chit who'd jilted him! Perhaps he needed someone more ... more experienced? Suddenly, caressing him with my quivering belly wasn't nearly enough!

I pulled a little way out of the clinch and took his cock in my questing fingers. He was like warm, moist suede stretched taut over a tempered steel core. I sighed. There was no hardness like a young man's hardness and I had the crazy urge to wank him to orgasm. I wanted to see his thick white juice come spurting out and fly across both our bodies. I wanted to drink his essence and massage it into my skin like some intimate elixir of youth.

My poise was in tatters now, and ideas of choreographing this lovemaking myself had flown clean out of the open window. One strong young hand closed tight around my bottom, and the other pushed boldly but gently between my legs. A finger entered my vagina, then swirled and probed and explored. I felt my clitoris twitch madly, then almost sigh in my slit as a smooth flat thumb settled firmly upon it and began slowly and demonically to rotate.

How could he know this was my favourite way of being touched? How could he know I liked tiny nibbling kisses at the same time? How could he know I was mellowed-out putty in his oh-so-sweet young hands! When his fingers left my sex, I chuntered like a kid losing its favourite toy.

But I cried out again, with awe this time, and pleasure, as he slid both his hands between my thighs and opened me wide, then took a rock-solid hold on my hips. Following his lead, I brought one leg up and across his pelvis, then let him lower me carefully on to his tool.

'Oh, Ross, Ross, Ross!' I babbled as he nudged into my wettened groove. How could he seem bigger than ever? Thicker and larger than life? As he pulled me downwards, he pushed his own body up – rising into my vagina like a great, smooth missile. I felt impaled, speared, stretched; mercilessly and wonderfully filled. His fingers dug deep in the flesh of my buttocks as he jammed me down harder than ever.

I was in the superior position and should've been in control. But it was this slender young god, prone beneath me, who had the true upper hand. He swung up into me with an imperious strength and force, using my own weight to get deeper inside me. Each plunge dragged deliciously on my clit, and tugged on some secret interior muscle that joined it directly to my womb and breasts. Crouched above him, I reached down to rub myself, just above his sliding cock, then opened my eyes to watch him watching me. He smiled, half smugly, half in wonder, then drove himself on and up right into my palpitating core.

I thought I might burst – then it seemed as if I did. My whole body was one collapsing, imploding mass, locked in a pleasure so intense the very moon and stars seemed to blaze like a fire in my loins.

Dazzled, I found myself slumped across Ross's chest, weeping and drooling, kissing his man-scented neck. His scream of ecstasy rippled beneath my lips, vibrating in his fine young throat as he surged and spurted inside me.

Minutes passed, and we settled down side by side, still half-entangled. Our bodies were all sticky and sweaty, but lying against him – still throbbing within – I felt irresistibly beautiful and young. In my heart of hearts I knew I wasn't technically either, but tomorrow would be the time to face facts.

I closed my eyes; closed out the facts and let love in.

'Amy?' His voice was faint, drowsy, still rough with sex. 'I feel better now. Much better.'

Snuggling closer, feeling better myself, I breathed in his sweetness and slept.

Studies in Red

OH, NO! Why now?

Lacey Hanlon sighed in the bathroom and studied the small splinter-shape of red that'd ruined all her plans.

Why now?

'Why not, dimbo?' she mocked in a whisper, 'It's your own fault for not keeping tabs on yourself in the first place!'

It *was* her own fault, true, but it didn't make things better. Why now? Just when the sexiest, most beautiful man she'd ever met had started putting out those unmistakable vibes. Why, when she'd been within gasping distance of making love with a man so talented and ideal he was almost a fantasy, had an old and not-very-trusted friend finally decided to arrive?

Goddammit! Why now?

'I've invited the artist to my party,' Jemma had said, 'He only lives upstairs.'

Lacey and her friend had been admiring the focal point of Jemma's new flat – a huge, bold and very passionate-looking abstract oil painting. It seemed to depict nothing in particular, yet to Lacey's eyes, it was surprisingly accessible. Painted by a man, it screamed out the concept of 'woman': robust yet strangely delicate, it was thickly daubed but scattered with small, intriguing areas of intricate unfathomable detail.

It's gorgeous! she'd thought, and still did.

So is he! she'd decided later on seeing the artist himself across the proverbial crowded room. Gorgeous, but not at all in the way she'd expected.

To Lacey the word 'artist' had always been synonymous with 'wimp'. It suggested a pale, long-haired, wild-eyed, limp-wristed aesthete.

Nathan Levay, however, was a muscular, jeans-clad hunk with steady, bright blue eyes, a rich, obviously natural tan, and an almost brutal squaddie-style haircut. He looked more like Rambo than Leonardo.

'You're kidding!' had been Lacey's comment when Jemma had pointed him out.

'Nope, that's the notorious Nathan: artistic genius and all round sex-god. If I wasn't engaged, Lace, I wouldn't let *you* anywhere near him! But as I am spoken for, I'll introduce you . . . Come on!'

Sadly, that first time, it'd been no big deal. Despite her own flaring response to the man, Lacey had detected no answering spark in him. He'd been quietly charming; but nothing more. They'd chatted a few minutes, then Lacey had drifted away, facing the fact that the notorious Nathan Levay was a good-natured, courteous and surprisingly modest man who didn't particularly fancy her. Which was somewhat unfortunate because over the next few weeks she'd spent nearly all her free time fantasizing about him.

At the damnedest moments, she'd see those bright blue eyes, then see them darken as her dream-self made him want her. She'd imagine herself clinging to those broad, muscular shoulders, her nails piercing his smooth, bronzed skin as he bore down strongly and entered her. Nights had been both the worst and the best of times. When she was only half awake, her interior videos were almost pornographic. She saw him naked, erect and about to love her; his brown body imposing, his penis long, hard, and thick. She smelt his male smell, tasted his skin and his sweat and his juices; then had him drink deeply of hers.

That won't happen now, she thought glumly. Not tonight, and probably not ever.

Although, when Jemma had announced this second party, Lacey had hoped . . . Boy, how she'd hoped! And she'd prepared herself for it with great care.

She'd fluffed out her brown-blonde curls into a full, soft cascade. She'd chosen clothes that flattered her trim body without being obvious: a white sailcloth mini-skirt and bomber jacket, a pretty white lace camisole. Her look was inviting but cool, flirtatious yet pristine. Now she felt none of those, because when she'd slipped away to the bathroom, she'd found out her period had started.

Being both confusingly irregular, and so busy she never kept track of herself anyway, Lacey could only thank her lucky stars there was a tampon amongst the junk in the depths of her handbag. It was a blessing, too, that she'd started feeling dizzy when she had. A few minutes more would've seen blood on her chic white skirt as well as her thin silk knickers. It was a bitter thing to happen just when Nathan had taken an interest.

He'd been deep in conversation with another girl when Lacey had first arrived, and observing him discreetly, she'd felt both furiously angry and acutely turned on. The bastard was looking even more luscious tonight than last time.

Denim seemed to be his uniform, and a faded 501 shirt was a perfect foil for his rugged good looks, its hazy washed-out colour only accentuating the electric blue brilliance of his eyes. Not that those eyes had seemed to notice Lacey. Not until a quarter of an hour ago, that was.

Already feeling wonky, she'd looked up suddenly from her depression and found the man of her dreams standing right in front of her: offering wine and a smile, and with seemingly lots to talk about. Within seconds, she'd felt herself bloom beneath his hot blue scrutiny, and found wit and sparkle from out of nowhere to match his subtle but sexy conversation.

He hadn't touched her, or said anything overtly suggestive, but tonight's Nathan seemed dangerously different. His eyes, his body language, and even the scent of him had changed. It was as if once noticing her, he'd marked her as his, then cut her out from the herd as his prey.

The idea of Nathan as a predator was deeply exciting to Lacey. Not to mention ironic. *She'd* wanted *him* from the very first moment. *She'd* already marked *him* as hers. Then this'd happened!

Feeling ungainly, unhappy and vaguely grubby, she started to insert the familiar white cotton tube – then groaned aloud in intense, unwanted pleasure. Her body spasmed as her feverish imagination made the small white cylinder into something much bigger and smoother and hotter – the stiff, heated bar of Nathan Levay's long prick!

'I thought you had run away,' he said softly when Lacey returned to the party five minutes later, her

131

face white and her hands shaking.

I should've done! she thought wildly, smiling and murmuring a vague excuse. It'd be much less painful to leave now – to weep, drink alone and masturbate – than to stay and be forced into embarrassing explanations.

'Thanks.' She took the fresh glass of wine he gave her, then drank it far faster than she'd intended.

Her body was actually hurting now, but she suspected the discomfort had more to do with frustration than periods. It was a primal but infuriating fact that when she bled, she always felt ten times as randy. Her body would crave sex like mad at precisely the moment a man was likely to turn tail and run in revulsion!

She'd read all the advice in the sex manuals: 'A truly sensual man won't be put off, etc . . .' but her own experiences didn't match the textbook. She'd always met with shudders of distaste, and even with the protecting barrier of a condom, no man had ever wanted her enough to enter a body that was bleeding. Worse still, it was usually the macho men – like Nathan Levay – who'd ended up being the most squeamish.

'Are you all right?' His soft voice cut clean through her pessimism

'Yes, I'm fine.'

In reality she felt terrible. Those fabulous eyes were so kind, so concerned. They only made things worse. For Lacey, gentleness was the most alluring quality a man could possess, a far stronger turn-on than looks, charm, achievements and suchlike. With a few words of tenderness alone, Nathan could've bedded her easily, but as he'd got everything else going for him as well, the sense of loss was so keen it was almost exquisite.

'You aren't fine at all, are you?' He took the empty glass from her hand, sending a shudder through the whole of her body.

Please don't! she shouted inside, wanting him more than ever.

'You look pale. Why don't we get out of here for a spell? It's too crowded . . . you might feel better if you can breathe.'

This was the moment. The moment when two people at a party had the potential to be two naked bodies entwined in a bed.

He only lived upstairs.

Don't do this! Lacey told herself, adoring the weight of his hand on her waist as he guided her from the room.

Please, Lacey, no! she pleaded inside as he pulled her against him on the stairs, the action slow and achingly gentle. Stop him now, you fool! she implored within as he cupped her head in one big, caressing hand and lowered his lips on to hers. She murmured incoherently, then voices physical and mental were silenced by the beauty of his warm, mobile mouth, and the moist pressure of his tongue as it slid between her conquered lips.

Lacey felt her stomach quicker and her vagina flutter around its small, inanimate obstruction. Some part of her was still worrying about blood, but a greater part was crying out for Nathan's strong male body. Her sex was calling out to be properly filled and her clitoris for the pressure of his flexible artist's fingers. Her breasts felt bursting and tender against his hard, denim-clad chest.

'I want you, Lacey,' he said as they drew apart, so he could open his front door. Desperate to explain, yet nervous beyond speech, she was powerless to do anything but be led like a lamb into his flat.

'I—' Her final protest was stifled when he placed one big hand lightly over her lips and used the other to press her smaller hand against his crotch. He was hot and massive beneath the denim.

I'll suck him! she decided in relief. Squeezing cautiously at his fine, hard bulge, she kissed the hand that lay across her lips. Fellatio wouldn't do much for her own frustration, but at least *she* could make love to *him*.

Nipping playfully at his fingers, she broke away, then sank to her knees before him, scrabbling at his heavy belt buckle. Taken by surprise, Nathan gasped aloud; but Lacey refused to be fazed and prised open his denims, pushing aside his shirt, and tugged down his white cotton briefs.

His prick was big, stiff and splendidly, throbbingly ready, it was as beautiful as Lacey had imagined and more – already slickly moist at the tip.

'You lovely, lovely girl!' he groaned, sweeping her hair away from her face himself as she dipped forward to take his glans in her mouth. Folding her lips around her teeth and sucking very slowly and carefully, she pulled at his jeans and underpants at the same time, wiggling them down his legs to his ankles. Cupping her fingers around his sleek, hard bottom, she could feel the muscles there tensing as his cock plunged repeatedly between her wet and working lips.

She knew this wasn't what he'd planned, but the thought of how tender Nathan *would've* been had an amazing effect on Lacey. Happy and relaxed, she felt her throat open and go loose, allowing him in far deeper than she'd ever taken a man before.

He was grunting steadily, his pleasure loud and uninhibited, when suddenly he froze to absolute stillness.

Isn't he going to come? thought Lacey, feeling thwarted. She kneaded his taut bottom encouragingly, then to her surprise and bewilderment, felt herself being prised gently off his cock.

'You're too good to me, you wonderful woman.' Nathan's voice was ragged, but his smile was determined. 'It's your turn now.'

'But—' Once again he stopped her complaints; this time with his lips, bending down to her with an astonishing grace considering he was still hobbled by his clothes.

And with that same grace, he quickly and efficiently stripped naked before her.

Even locked in her panic, Lacey had to gasp in awe at the fabulous condition of his body. Strongly but not grotesquely muscled, he was a perfect blend of power, strength and long-limbed elegance. His skin was a glossy toasted gold, and though his chest was smooth and hair-free, his pubic area was densely flossed with black.

Completely nude, he knelt down beside her and pressed the full length of his bare body against her clothed one.

'I know what's bothering you,' he murmured into the tangle of her hair.

'You don't,' she said through gritted teeth, torn between ecstasy and horror as he cupped her breast through its thin silken covering.

'I do!' He pushed down the flimsy garment, took her nipple between his long, nimble fingers. 'You've got your period and you think it'll put me off.'

'I . . . Yes. That's it,' she babbled, falling against him, seeking the comfort of his warmth and solidity.

And yet, she still felt terror. She could feel the ripple of blood inside her, see its redness in her mind's-eye, while everything around them looked

135

so white and unmarked.

The rug they crouched on was white. Her clothes were white. Even golden-skinned Nathan, though darker, was immaculate in his naked peerless beauty. 'But it doesn't matter, my sweet.' His voice was soft as his hand slid up her thigh and cradled her silk-covered crotch. 'I'm a painter. I'm always daubed with colour . . . My hands get covered with it. So does most of the rest of me, given the way I work.' She couldn't see him grinning but she could hear it. She thought of Jemma's painting, then imagined its creation. Nathan moulding the pigment in place with his hands – his fingers, arms, face and chest all smeared not only with red, but with a whole pallette of other colours too.

'It'll get everywhere,' she whispered, then groaned with pleasure as Nathan's pressing palm rotated. Slowly. 'And I haven't got any more—' His lips covered hers, his exploring tongue pushing away all doubts and all inconvenient lacks.

'Don't worry,' he said when he'd subdued both her mouth and her body. Limp as a doll, Lacey felt herself whisked up in his arms, and then being carried into his bedroom and placed in the centre of a large bed. A bed with a milk white chenille bedspread. 'Relax,' he went on, kissing her cheek, his superb body looming over her briefly before he strode away towards the door, 'My sister stays here sometimes. She'll have left everything you need.'

In his absence, Lacey dreamed because she didn't want to think; or worry. Rolling luxuriantly on the soft white bedcover, she kicked off her shoes and shuffled out of her jacket. Would Nathan want to take the rest off himself? Still in her short skirt, with her thin lace top still pushed down off one breast, she followed his instructions and relaxed. Pressing her hand to her belly, she felt one kind of ache recede and another, better one, grow strong. As it did, Nathan appeared in the doorway, then walked, magnificent, towards her.

He dropped a selection of objects on to the bed at her side: fluffy white towels, tissues, packets of condoms and tampons, a drum full of scented wipes.

'There! Everything we need,' he said with a smile, dropping himself amongst the paraphernalia and lying down beside her.

Lacey stroked the long gleaming flank of the most beautiful male body she'd ever seen, then started helping Nathan undress her.

It began with a lot of giggling and squirming and shuffling on her part as they manoeuvred with clothes and towels. Then Nathan explored and stroked and soothed her. Gentle and encouraging, his mouth moved and murmured against her throat as he coaxed her into the final, crucial preparation. A careful tug on the small blue cord that dangled between her wantonly parted thighs. Lacey had one single clear jolt of fear, then forgot it completely as deft fingers plunged her into her crimson wetness and started to make magic and art.

Within seconds she was coming. Whimpering like a child as her body experienced shocks of pleasure from the touch of her clitoris under Nathan's large, flat and delicately circling thumb.

'I love you!'

Crying out spontaneously, Lacey arched against him, pressing her red-smeared flesh against his hand, 'Oh God, yes, I love you!' Clinging on for dear life, bucking and heaving with bliss, she was dimly aware that it wasn't Nathan alone she so suddenly loved. Yes, she did love *him*, but she also loved herself and her own bleeding body – regardless of the mess it was making!

Blood was everywhere in seconds. In between massaging her to climax after climax, Nathan took up the bright fluid on his fingers and literally painted on her with it. Just a few slight strokes of his genius, and she had birds on her belly, flowers on her face, and butterflies streaming across her breasts.

He decorated himself too. Bold red slashes made him into a crew-cut Indian brave, then all their adornments were smudged to abstraction as he shimmied himself against her, laughing with erotic glee.

It should've been gory, but instead it was only glorious.

Like painted savages, they frolicked and fondled and fooled with each other. As each delight blended into the next, Lacey could no longer keep a count of all the sensual acts they'd shared and the number of times that Nathan had made her come. It seemed that the whole of her body and mind had denatured and reformed into one immense, sublime, and flaming scarlet orgasm.

Everything was beautiful, everything was sacred and right, even her blood. Her blood on his cock; her blood on his mouth as he looked up from kissing her trembling belly and smiled.

'Why the sudden change? Why tonight?' Lacey asked later, in the shower, as Nathan sluiced his studies in red from her body.

'Because you looked vulnerable tonight. Pale and pure ... Like a canvas I could paint on.' He skimmed the streaming flow from her hips and thighs, its colour faintly pink but clearing rapidly.

138

'And now you've painted . . .' Lacey held her breath. 'What next?'

'This!' he whispered, sweeping his arms around her squeaky clean body and clasping it to the strong, hard length of his, 'The painting was fine. But it's the canvas underneath I want to keep.' His voice was low and almost shaky, but clearly audible through the steady hiss of the shower.

'Keep? What do you mean "keep"?' Earlier, in orgasm, she'd told him she loved him; but now she knew it was true.

'Just what I said . . .'

'For how long?' He was making patterns on her back with the water now, but to Lacey he was painting with fire on her soul and drawing out their future on her own wet skin.

'As long as you want to stay, my love,' Nathan said softly, tilting up her face for a kiss, 'How about forever?'

Quiet Storm

AT LAST, A real, nice, honest, beautiful man to have sex with.

I'd had that thought, a month ago, when Bryn Stevens had first joined our unit – and I was still having it now, even after four weeks of his total indifference.

Well, that's not exactly true. Bryn had been civil and almost friendly towards me in all our workaday dealings; it was only when the wind blew even vaguely in the direction of sex that he seemed to cool right off. Which was a bit of a problem because I was in a heatwave for him!

I hadn't felt like this in ages. Since my last relationship, I'd been stuck in the sexual doldrums. I hated casual flings and there didn't seem to be anyone around to get in deeper with. I just didn't fancy anybody enough.

Until Bryn walked – or should I say limped – his way into my life. Our new training officer was a modern classic: a tall, dark and sensitive hunk with above-average intelligence and eyes as grey as thunderclouds. It was the idiosyncrasies, though, the deviations from the norm, which made him so irresistibly wantable. He had a rangy, understated strength and a fit man's poise and composure, but it was his barely detectable limp that set him apart as special, vulnerable and different.

It was the same with his moods. His confidence and charm made him a very desirable companion and an accomplished and effective trainer. He was especially good at teaching women, and his off-the-cuff jokes and perfectly judged light-hearted flirting made them far more relaxed and liable to learn than a strictly conventional training style would've done.

He seemed to get along well with his colleagues too. He was nothing short of dynamic in team situations and his ideas were always exciting. But sometimes, just sometimes, when on the surface he was at his most smiling and agreeable, I'd spot this 'otherness' in there too: a kind of storm in the back of his eyes; a discreet but palpable rage that was as puzzling as it was elusive. The strangest thing of all was that it often seemed directed at me. What had I done? I wondered. Except fancy the man something rotten.

But I hadn't been obvious about it; that's not my way. I'd been helpful but not pushy; friendly and approachable but not forwrad. All in all, I couldn't figure out why I was getting these occasional but turbulent black looks. I'm no great beauty, I know, but some men would've been quite pleased to get my attentions . . .

Patsy Colvin doesn't give up easily, however, so without making a major deal of it I set out to get the low-down on the mercurial Mr Stevens. The divisional grapevine yielded swift and intriguing fruit . . .

Eighteen months ago, Bryn had been all set to

establish his own training company – a fact which didn't surprise me given his skills – but just before the final negotiations, he'd had a serious motorbike accident. He'd been in hospital for several months and in consequence his business had folded without ever seeing the light of day – which explained why he was stuck in the backwoods of local government training rather than having a high-profile enterprise of his own. The accident also explained his limp, and the intense physiotherapy and rehabilitation he must've needed afterwards accounted for his superb state of fitness now.

It didn't explain everything, though . . . A certain amount of professional frustration was natural and understandable, but where did the personal resentment come from, the distinct but furious animosity I sensed when Bryn looked at me?

Armed with this scant background knowledge I decided to re-double my efforts. I had my blonde hair cut and restyled, I went on a diet, and I invested in several smart but understated new 'work' suits. I went about my campaign calmly and quietly and although it might've been my imagination, I did seem to start making some headway.

I began masturbating again too. Those erotic doldrums had become a high pressure area now, and one night, after spending the whole day wondering why Bryn wouldn't make a pass at me, I started stroking my clitoris while I thought of him.

No stranger to the joys of self-pleasure, I even dug out my vibrator; a sleek, quiet toy that I'd played with quite a bit in the past and suddenly felt a great need for now.

This time, though, I didn't use pictures from my favourite magazines to get myself going. It was Bryn in my mind as I rubbed myself lightly with my fingers; Bryn as I switched on my vibrant electric friend and skimmed it over my sex. It was Bryn flicking at me and teasing me as the thick pleasure-giving cylinder slid rudely into my body. I didn't usually bother with insertion, but now it seemed a good way to simulate a cock. With the help of a smooth, slightly warm vibrator I could imagine Bryn's hot, pulsing erection inside me and I cried out his name as I climaxed.

Matters came to a head of sorts when, as a team, we all went swimming in our lunch-hour. I was pleased with my slimming attempts because my blue and white stripey swimsuit looked even more flattering than I'd hoped. I got plenty of admiring looks, but unfortunately not from the quarter I wanted.

The man himself looked fabulous, as I'd expected. His body was long, lean and olivey-brown, with muscles that spoke of many gruelling hours in the gym. And he filled out his sleek black Speedo trunks to perfection!

Even his scars seemed sexy: a criss-crossing of thin, pink puckered lines that girdled his lower back and dipped mysteriously beneath the dark shiny surface of his swimtrunks. Whatever had happened to him must've hurt like hell, and I felt a sudden urge to nurture. It was weird, but I couldn't stop wishing I'd known him much sooner and been able to nurse him back to health; been the one who'd restored him to his sex life . . . That black Speedo left nothing to the imagination. As I back-stroked through the water, I fantasized about other kinds of strokings: the long searching glide of Bryn's fingers on my body; the slow, steady pump of his cock as it stroked its way deep into my sex.

He was a superb swimmer, and seemed to be

143

having fun; until – inevitably! – he caught me ogling his thinly covered crotch. That changed everything. A look of black rage crossed his water-jewelled face and he whirled away and threw himself into the deep end for a series of fast and punishing laps that effectively cut him off from the rest of us.

Strangely enough, he was okay with me afterwards, and at work, but I couldn't help noticing that frown again when we found out that he and I had to work together on a new training pack. It was a rush job that'd been outstanding for far too long, and there was no way we could meet our deadline without taking it home to finish it. Together.

I tried to stay cool and remember it was just routine and that he didn't particularly like me, but as I let him into my flat and we spread out the materials on the coffee-table, I couldn't keep my soaring spirits down. It was deadly boring stuff – a Health and Safety Training Course the unit was hoping to market – but even so Bryn attacked it with his usual competence and enthusiasm, and in spite of the peculiar 'edge' between us, he soon made the whole thing seem fascinating – even worth getting worked up about.

Not that I wasn't worked up already. I'd seen Bryn in a suit, and in his swimming trunks, but not in anything more 'in between'. In jeans and a soft, lambswool sweater, he was even more mouthwatering than ever, and I was soon paying far less attention to safety regulations than I was to his strong, serious face and his lean, die-hard body. Especially the portion concealed behind the faded blue denim at his groin. I kept thinking about how distracting it'd looked in black lycra . . . and when I got up to demonstrate a trip hazard for one of the pack's illustrations, it was hardly surprising I actually went headlong. It was unintentional, I swear it was, but I ended up in Bryn's arms in a classic *Gone with the Wind* clinch.

I've always believed in the power of wishful thinking, and as I looked up into his fine grey eyes, I decided to test out my theories. I hoped. I willed. I silently begged him to kiss me.

And he did.

It was a long kiss, and thorough. A kiss that engaged the whole of his firm, assertive mouth and his mobile, flexible tongue. I responded gallantly and in kind, thrilled to bits that he was just as powerful, sexy and masterful as I'd hoped for.

Happy as a sand-girl, I breezed straight into the next stage. Though his lips were sensual, Bryn's hands seemed strangely reticent. Taking the initiative, I passed searching fingers tentatively across his crotch . . . and suddenly I was on the floor again!

He'd dumped me; all but dropped me. Plunging down from the dreamy heights of the kiss, I found myself sitting on the rug and furiously angry.

'What the hell is it, Bryn?' I demanded, my body as thwarted as my mind. We'd been so close. So ready. 'What's the matter? I thought you liked me . . . I thought you might even be getting round to *wanting* me?'

He was on his feet now, turning away, his straight body hunched as if in pain.

'I do like you, Patsy. And I'd *like* to want you.' Where was the authority in his voice now, the confidence? He was whispering almost, and not making sense at all.

'What do you mean "like to want"? You either do or you don't.'

'It's not that simple,' he said, turning back

towards me, and for one second, looking downwards. Towards his undisturbed groin ... 'I'm impotent, Patsy. A damp squib. I can't get it up.'

In some ways it was the scariest moment of my life, but I didn't feel either revulsion, panic or pity. What I still felt was desire. I was turned on for him and filled with a strange, new, almost missionary zeal. Okay, so we couldn't fuck ... But what else could we do?

'I had an accident. I suppose you know.' Slowly, wearily, he sank down on the settee, then pulled me up from the floor to sit with him. 'Some nerves in my back and pelvis were damaged. Everything else got back to normal, but sadly ...' raising his slender right hand, he waggled a finger forlornly, 'not that.' He sighed and let his hand fall to his long, denim-covered thigh. 'I know it's not an excuse, but that's why I've been so "off" with you, Patsy. Every time I look at you, I realise just exactly what I've lost.'

He smiled then: a soft, wry, very beautiful little-boy smile. At that, my stubborn, determined streak flowed out into a mile-wide river. I reached out and took his hand, folding my own fingers around the one he'd used to demonstrate his deficiency.

'Look, do you know for certain it ... it doesn't work any more? Have you tried?'

'Yes, I had a whole series of embarrassing tests and there wasn't even a flicker.' The smile turned sad, and there was a bitter twist to his sexy kissable mouth. 'I'm sorry, Patsy. There's nothing I'd like more than to be able to make love to you.' His fingers moved in my grasp, swivelling neatly until he was able to stroke my hand and caress it smoothly, delicately and gently. He hardly seemed aware of what he was doing.

'But what about feeling?' I was getting ideas now. Bold, outrageous, exciting ideas. 'Even if you can't get hard, do you still have . . . um . . . sensations?'

'I don't know. I've never thought about it.' When he looked up, I could see he was following my meaning. His eyes were bright, almost wild. 'I've been too pissed off with my body to investigate the situation . . . Too angry.'

'Let's investigate now then.' Bold as brass, I reached for the belt of his jeans.

'Are you sure?' He put his hand over mine and stilled it, but I sensed that he didn't really want to stop me.

'Yes! What have we got to lose?' I wasn't quite the hotshot trainer that Bryn was, but in my own way I was no mean motivator. Personal development had always been my special forte. 'If nothing happens for you at least you'll've tried. And as for me, well, there's nothing wrong with your hands, is there? Or your mouth?' Even as I said it, it dawned on me what I'd *really* always liked best in bed anyway!

Bryn didn't answer. Instead, he prised my fingers gently from his jeans . . . and started undressing me.

He was deft and efficient, as he was in all things; as each garment came off, he caressed the area it'd covered. There was no panic, no fumbling, just grace and pure, sensual enjoyment. His fingertips were beneficent yet probing, skipping lightly over ticklish areas and pressing harder at the parts that cried out for it. When my breasts were naked, he cupped them, one in each hand, and pressed his face between them, his hot breath a pleasure in itself. His faint evening stubble was deliciously abrasive; as if sensing this, he smoothed his cheeks across my nipples, one after the other, again and again and again.

147

'Oh, yes!' I sobbed, loving the sensation both for itself and for its effect between my legs. I tried to pull off my panties, but again, he stopped my efforts and supplanted them with his. Sliding away the inhibiting white cotton, he tossed it aside, then opened my slit with his fingers.

'Hey, you!' I gasped as his thumb flicked at my clitoris. 'You've still got your clothes on. This's as much for you as for – Oh, oh God! Aaagh!'

I'd wanted him for four weeks and it didn't take much to make me come. A couple of tiny experimental strokes with his thumb-tip and the whole of my wet, needy sex was in motion. For a blank, timeless moment, I completely forgot what I'd been going to say, or even think. All I could do was babble and moan and sob while Bryn coaxed orgasm after orgasm after orgasm out of me with his sweet and rhythmical petting.

When I stopped shouting, he laid me tenderly back against the cushions and pushed my sweat-soaked hair off my brow. I grinned up at him, still panting, my thighs lolling apart and my happy sex gaping and pouting.

'Now you, mister,' I said, feeling wonderful.

'We don't need to,' he faltered. 'It'll be one helluva non-event. There'll be nothing for *you*, Patsy . . .' He reached down and cupped his groin, flashing me that beautiful juvenile smile again.

'I still want to try.' I was already tugging at his jumper.

He stopped fighting and succumbed to me, his actions more hopeful than his words had been; especially when I brushed against his nipple with the jumper and got an appreciative 'ooh' in response. I touched him there again when his chest was bare and he shuddered with an unfeigned delight.

'Good?' I queried, feeling hopeful myself now.

'Very,' he purred, holding my fingertips in place with his own.

'How about elsewhere? Any action?'

''Fraid not.' He shrugged, and his chest and shoulders glistened like satin.

'Not to worry. We'll keep trying, shall we?'

I was enjoying myself in a different way now to when he'd touched me, but curiously the feelings were equally as exalted. His body was sculpted and magnificent, strangely whole in spite of the wounds it'd suffered. I loved the texture of his skin, the hardness and the cut of his physique; and it was this, and the courage it'd taken to get fit again, that defined him absolutely as a man . . . and not the organ that hung down between his legs.

When he was stripped to his underpants, he hesitated. 'I might as well keep them on. Nothing's happening.' He reached out towards me, ready to take me in his arms and start caressing me again.

But I'd made my mind up. 'No, let me see you. You're not scarred there are you?'

'No. Not at all!' He grinned ruefully. 'It looks fine. It just doesn't work anymore ... '

His cock was as good to look at as the rest of him. A thick, pleasing length of flesh, circumcised, dark plummy red and nestling in a wiry forest of near-black pubic hair. I allowed myself one single wistful imagining of what might have been, then it was *my* turn to push *him* back against the cushions. I half hoped he might spring to life when I touched him, but willing as I was, no miracles occured. His penis felt alive and hot, and the skin of it was like fluid velvet, but as I handled him he remained quite inert.

At least his cock did. Bryn himself stirred on the couch, moving his limbs luxuriantly and making low sounds of pleasure in his throat. There was still no sign of an erection, but as I stroked him, it was obvious *something* was happening. I hardly dare ask what he was feeling . . . but suddenly he spoke up, letting his thighs fall open as he did so.

'That's good. So good. I didn't realise . . .'

Empowered by his praise, I set two hands to my task – one tracing the contours of his soft spongy shaft while the other went exploring and voyaging.

I caressed his nipples, his belly and his thighs. Then, as my confidence increased, I went in between the rounds of his buttocks, tickling him naughtily and urging him to tilt his hips. As he sighed and obediently lifted himself, I reached past his balls and touched his perineum and the rose of his anus. He was moaning quietly but continuously now, swirling his pelvis, still flaccid but in all other ways clearly excited.

As I stroked at his tight male hole, and tickled him there, there was the faintest of responses in his cock. The soft chunky organ seemed to ripple in my grasp, and when I pushed more daringly and my finger went right inside him, I felt him throb, then throb again, while moisture oozed thickly from the tip of his cock.

'Oh, please . . . Please . . .' he burbled and I pressed in deeper, feeling for the gland I knew was there but had never sought out before. When I found it he cried out softly, edging his body forward, inviting me to caress him from within.

It was new territory, an unknown land, but so obviously and wonderfully a pleasure zone. I wiggled my fingertip inside him; I massaged and rubbed and blindly circled . . . and within seconds he was jerking like a puppet, shouting and whining, his whole body trembling in my hold. His soft cock fluttered in my fingers like a captive bird and as I looked down, fascinated, it annointed my palm with a veil of silvery fluid.

It was such a small, inconspicuous event, but I sensed that its significance was awesome. As I slid my finger out of him, Bryn rolled sideways and away from me, curling into a ball, a huddle, a foetus. After a couple of seconds, I realised to my horror he was crying – really sobbing his heart out, his strong frame shaking in a great, quiet storm of weeping that terrified me right to the core.

He'd been injured. I'd gone too far. I'd hurt him . . .

But when he unfurled his long limbs again and sat up awkwardly in front of me, his face was as bright as an angel's.

'That was beautiful, Patsy. I never thought I'd feel all that again.' He scrubbed at his eyes with those narrow, graceful fingers of his, then grinned shame-faced. 'I don't know what to say.'

'You don't need to say anything.' I was thunder-struck myself. Overwhelmed. I wanted to kiss Bryn and hug him, do everything all over again for the sheer joy of seeing and feeling his climax. But first I had needs of my own. 'There're some things *you* could do. When you've got your breath back . . .'

I touched my fingers to his, and when our eyes met, his twinkled knowingly. He'd got my drift, and my pussy was already tingling. I looked at his clever, expressive hands and the generous promise of his mouth. I looked at his slumbering cock and thought how fine-textured and silky its skin was and how much I enjoyed just touching it. I thought about all the lovely, languorous things that Bryn and I could do together, and I smiled.

I'd been right after all. I *had* found a real, nice, honest, beautiful man to have sex with!

Perfecto

'TEARS AGAIN?' ASKED a soft, velvet-gentle voice.

I emerged blearily from my misery and craving and saw a crisply folded handkerchief being held out towards me.

'Yes . . . Oh, dear . . . I'm sorry . . .' I took the perfect white square and dabbed at my eyes with it. It was embarrassing me always blubbing like this; she'd only been here a week and this was the fourth time she'd caught me crying . . .

'Care to talk about it?' that soothing voice enquired again, and I looked up mournfully from the already mangled hankie to the pale, concerned face of its owner.

Maria Samuels was *supposed* to be my new personal assistant, but with me like this, she was already shouldering almost all the office workload. I was luckier than I deserved that those slender shoulders were more than up to it . . .

'Look, Sylvie,' she said quietly, 'I've been watching you. You're upset. Why don't you tell me what's wrong? I know we don't know each other too well, but I'd like to help.'

Yeah, she'd been watching me all right. I'd felt

those steady, penetrating eyes on me a lot during the past week. When I wasn't pining for Peter, that was.

They were beautiful eyes too, I realised as she sat down beside me and placed an immaculately manicured hand on my arm.

She was right. I needed to tell someone. But I'd been so wound up in Peter for so long, there *was* no-one . . . Except her.

So out it came. The story of Peter and me. The story of a capable successful woman acting like a sex-enslaved bimbo over a man who was divine in bed but a selfish, ten-timing monster everywhere else . . . Once I'd started, I couldn't stop. Amongst the sobs and hiccups, I blurted out things I'd never told anybody. How if Peter smiled that filmstar smile of his I was putty. How he'd make me beg for more of his perfect *Joy of Sex* fucking. How he'd make me climax in a way so expert I half expected a judge to pop up and give marks for technical merit. And how afterwards – while my body still sizzled – I'd wish I hadn't been so 'easy' . . .

Maria sat through it: her eyes knowing but not disapproving, her fine oval face composed, almost nun-like. Until I started on the let-downs, the broken dates, the sightings with other women; the fact that even now, I still jumped when he whistled. Then, through a fresh batch of tears, I saw her change. Her deep, dark, golden-hazel eyes flashed with righteous female rage; yet her gently husky voice revealed nothing of it.

'Don't you think you've taken enough?' she said evenly, patting at her smooth, shimmering hair. It was that gesture that gave her away. I'd seen it several times when she was nervous or stressed. While thinking hard, her fingers would flick

gracefully to her lovely streaked-chestnut bob –
adjust a strand or two – yet never upset its flawless
geometric styling.

'Yes. No. Oh, I don't know . . . I'm always like this
in relationships! I'm great at business: I love pulling
the strings at work. But when it comes to love and
sex and stuff, I'm hopeless! It's my nature, Maria. I
can't help it. I feel so ashamed, so out of control. I
wouldn't mind being this way if Peter wasn't such a
total shit! If someone nice took charge I'd be in
seventh heaven . . .'

'So the gist of it is' – she took the hankie and
folded it into a neat white square again – 'tonight's
your anniversary of sorts, and he's leaving you
alone and completely miserable?'

I nodded glumly. She was right: I was pathetic.

'Well you won't be!' Something foreign and
powerful glinted in her eyes then, and suddenly I
felt . . . felt scared. And excited too.

'You're going out with me tonight, Sylvie – to a
club I know, called "Perfecto". And you're going to
have an absolutely wonderful time!'

'But—'

'No buts! Trust me!' Her eyes flashed again, and
her mouth – small, rosy and perfectly sculpted –
curved into a smile so determined that my heart
lurched heavily inside me, 'You like being taken
charge of, don't you?'

I nodded again, feeling peculiarly light-headed.

'Well then! I'm taking charge!'

Later, as I got ready, then made my way to the
pre-arranged meeting place, the second thoughts
began to arrive.

For a start, I'd never been one for 'girlie' nights
out: Chippendales and suchlike. And that club –

Perfecto – the name rang a vague bell. It was notorious for something, but for what, I couldn't for the life of me remember.

And another thing: I hardly knew anything about Maria!

Oh, her CV was peerless and her references irreproachable. She was superb at her job, but as a woman – an unknown quantity. All I did know, I realised with a sudden flush of confusion, was that she was quite exquisitely lovely to look at!

Not in an obvious way: that milky complexion and those even, sculpted features were only ever oh-so-lightly made up, and her conservative clothes were aptly matched by her immaculately kept hair, her discreetly polished nails and her generally impeccable grooming.

Yet, even as I catalogued these virtuous and commendable features, I recognised certain others: subversive ones that made me blush – furiously.

Beneath all that bandbox perfection was an equally perfect figure. She had full, voluptuous breasts, a sylph-slim waist and a long, inviting throat which seemed to demand that someone kiss it.

I didn't know why I was thinking things like that, but if Ms Samuels was so gorgeous, it seemed a waste that she go out with me!

Turning a corner, I checked my bearings. Half way down the street ahead was a lighted frontage and discreet neon signs, 'Perfecto'.

Then it hit me.

Several things hit me.

First, Maria was nowhere to be seen, although she'd promised she'd be here waiting. Second, I remembered why Perfecto was notorious.

There were people out on the pavement; people

laughing and drinking and boogie-ing to the dancebeats wafting from the open door; women boogie-ing – *only* women.

Perfecto was a gay club and it was 'ladies night'! I turned away, gathering myself to run . . .

'Hello, Sylvie,' a voice murmured and I turned back towards the club and the women. A slim figure detached itself from the shadows and I realised Maria really *had* arrived first.

But not the Maria I'd expected.

She was still faultlessly turned out. Her dinner jacket – a man's – was cut like a dream. Her leather jeans were soft, gleaming and fitted like a second skin. Her shirt was as pristine as the ones she wore for work, but made of silk crêpe, open almost to the waist, and revealing just as white and dazzling in its long inviting vee.

She smiled – half archly, half shyly – and patted her sleekly gelled hair. The gesture was familiar, but this was not the Maria Samuels who functioned so efficiently in the office, and who listened so quietly and calmly. This was another Maria: one who made my pulse run riot and the hair on the back of my neck stand up. To say she unnerved me was an understatement!

'Come on, Sylvie . . . Don't look like that! I won't bite!' She laughed richly but kindly, then took my arm and led me towards Perfecto.

Earlier in the day her fingers had been cool and consoling on my arm, but now they were like strands of flame. Suddenly I was sweaty and breathless, and my head swam with her perfume. She smelt spicy-sweet and musky, the fragrance so strong and heady I could almost see it. At the club door she produced banknotes from her back pocket with a bravura flourish, and we passed like VIPs

156

through a phalanx of smiling, sociable women. Someone called out, 'Hi, Sam! Looking good tonight! Who's your sexy friend?' and Maria turned like a visiting goddess and blew her admirer a kiss.

'S . . . Sam?' I stammered, letting her steer me to a table and sit me down like a child on a teashop outing.

'People call me that.' Her eyes were sultry and oblique, glittering in the subdued light. 'People who like me.' She turned away, signalled for a drink and I caught myself panting.

There was nothing subtle about her now; nothing understated at all. She stunned me with her fabulous cleavage, her berry-stained mouth and her Nefertiti eyes. I felt helpless and wasted, but this time I liked it. She was weird; she was outrageous; but I still felt safe. I had an overpowering urge to call her 'Sam'.

'Okay, I know what you're thinking – about this . . .' She gestured to the women around us, all so at home in their own milieu. 'About me. And you're not wrong.' Her fingers fluttered expressively, then settled on my wrist like a bird. 'But no-one here expects anything of you. Least of all me. All I want is you to relax and be happy. No strings. No pressure. Understand?'

I nodded, then with my heart thrashing in my chest, I turned my hand so hers could settle in it. 'Yes, Sam, I understand.'

Her smile washed across me like a voodoo ray. 'Great! Now let's have some fun!'

And we did. I should've felt uncomfortable in a place so far out of my own experience, but I didn't. Sam – for that was how I had to think of her – was a star in this sky, and even though I was a stranger, I too was bathed in her radiance. With her I felt free and relaxed, controlled yet happy and at ease. The women we talked and drank and danced with were friendly, but there was no pressure.

Except the pressure within. The pressure I wanted. I knew what was happening when she led me to the dance-floor . . .

She moved like a fury, all fire and lissom grace; as I watched, possessed, and tried to move with her, I felt sex jolt heavily in my belly. The same sweet tug I'd felt for Peter, a thousand years ago. It kicked harder than ever now, here in Perfecto, and I was felled like a tree – slain by my divine, different Sam. I was snared by her long, long thighs, so sensual in that thin, dark leather; by her full breasts, swinging proud and bra-less in her cloud of a shirt. As the dance became wilder, she discarded her jacket and showed me more: nipples flirting free as she stretched and swayed, twin red points, stiff and fruity – as dear and kissable as her soft, tinted lips.

We said little to each other – the music was too loud – but we made jokes with our eyes and our faces. We made contact, found meaning, and I felt myself alter. Irrevocably.

'I told you. I don't expect anything,' she said, later, as we crept into her flat.

She didn't look quite so immaculate now, not nearly so perfect. Her shirt clung darkly to her swollen nipples; her fringe was wet and ruffled; her body smelt strongly of leather and sweat and sex. Yet still, with no conscious effort at all, she controlled me.

'Neither do I.' My voice was tiny, my wanting huge. 'But I'd like . . . I . . .'

I didn't know what words to use but Sam heard me all the same. 'Oh God, yes, yes . . .' she breathed as her lips pressed down on mine and her hands enclosed my yearning breasts.

She had a big squashy sofa in the middle of her living room, and as she lowered us on to it, she kept hold of my flesh; kneaded and stroked through my thin silk top . . . Then the silk was gone and she was rubbing my uncovered skin, pulling my nipples, twisting and fondling them with a joy that passed right through my squirming body and gathered in my hungering clit.

'Yes, I know! I know!' she murmured, sliding to her knees and wedging the heel of one hand in my crotch and the other hand under my bottom. 'It hurts, my baby. It hurts, doesn't it,' she cooed, rocking me on her palms; working my cleft from back and front. 'It needs rubbing, my angel, doesn't it? Rubbing and loving and kissing?'

I started to say 'yes, it does', but grunted obscenely when she invaded my panties, then stripped them away and fingered my naked sex.

'Hold your breasts, Sylvie!' she whispered, 'Caress your nipples and it'll feel even better.'

It did. I pinched my own teats, mauled my own body, and felt my legs fall open and my clit rise to her maurauding touch. She wasn't gentle, as I'd expected; she was rough and frenzied and it was exactly what I wanted and needed. She pounded my clitoris, jerked it to and fro between her fingertips, then left it high and dry for three long, cruel seconds . . . I whined like an animal on heat, and in that instant, her beautiful face was between my thighs. Her nuzzling lips caught my bead of lust, and then she was sucking, sucking, sucking and I was screaming, screaming, screaming as a great bowl of light uptipped in my crotch and poured on and out through the whole of my flailing body.

*

159

The next day, Peter phoned. Puzzled. His plans had changed last night. He'd called me. I read effortlessly between the lines. He'd needed sex; his new floozy had let him down; but there was always ever faithful, ever available Sylvie, wasn't there?

I listened to the spiel, the same old song, and smiled down from a new and blissful height. He started to complain, but other, more appealing sounds attract me: the office door closing softly; the catch falling; light, even steps crossing the room towards me . . .

My heart sings. My loins churn deliciously. A soft hand falls like grace on my shoulder. My perfect one moves to stand before me and my lips form a silent, rapturous greeting. We've only been apart since the small hours, but it seems like an aeon since we last caressed.

Sartorial as ever, she's everything that's wonderful to my eyes. It's 'financier' pin-stripe this morning, not sweat-soaked silk and leather. But still she looks otherly, remarkable, potent. Without words, she's already taken charge. I make as if to end my call, to end Peter-in-my-life by the simple act of putting down the phone, but she shakes her head and grins.

There's a fire in her this morning! Her lips shine; her gel-smoothed hair shines; and her sweet soul blazes in her eyes like a burning torch to lead me from the darkness. She moves closer and closer as Peter starts to wheedle; she lifts my skirt as he asks, aggrieved, why I wasn't available last night.

'Who are you seeing?'

'No-one you know.'

I gasp as 'no-one' slides her fingers into my panties . . .

'Where did you go?'

'None of your business,' I say, my knuckles white on the receiver handle. Between my legs, the heat and pleasure are 'none of his business' either . . .

'Who is it?' he demands.

'Sam!' I cry, looking straight into her awesome, beloved face.

'And where did you go with this "Sam"?' persists Peter, angry and desperate. 'Where the hell did you go?'

'To Perfecto!' I sob.

'To Perfecto, Perfecto, Perfecto!' I scream, freed forever as I come at the hand of my magical saviour.

The Old Uno Due

I WAS STARKERS when the doorbell rang, and it was a condition I wasn't too pleased about. Surely Ollie wasn't here already? It was only mid-afternoon and my wine and pizza welcome night wasn't due to start until seven at the earliest. I shouldn't have felt cross, I know, but there's nothing worse than being caught on the hop when you want all your preparations to be perfect. Poor old Ollie had been having such a rough time lately, I really wanted this evening to be a treat.

'You're far too early!' I cried, flinging the flat door wide open . . .

A split second later, I slammed it shut again, feeling a complete and utter fool. It hadn't *been* Ollie on the doorstep, getting an eyeful from the gaping neckline of my robe. It'd been the two tall, dark and handsome not-quite-strangers who lived in the flat upstairs; the Italian brothers, Pietro and Paulo di Something or Other, whom I'd been fancying – as unobtrusively as I could – since they'd moved in a couple of months ago.

'I'm sorry about that,' I muttered when I opened the door again, my bathrobe securely sashed across my naked and still damp breasts. 'I don't usually slam the door in my neighbours' faces. But I was expecting someone else and you gave me a shock.'

'I am very sorry if we frightened you, Signorina Foxton,' said the taller one, Pietro, who spoke such exceedingly good English that his diction was better than mine was, 'but we have a serious problem and we would be very grateful if you could help us.'

How could I resist? Not only was he so polite and roguishly woebegone that my feminine heart melted instantly, he was also one of the most handsome bits of stuff I'd ever had the pleasure of setting eyes on. Ditto, his brother.

There they stood on my doorstep, two raven-haired, chocolate-eyed charmers. One was taller and wiry, the other slightly shorter and muscular; but both were gorgeous in snow-white T-shirts which showed off their olive complexions, and tight blue jeans which clung to their slim hips, their long thighs, and their deliciously well-formed crotches. What red-blooded woman wouldn't have wanted to help them?

'Come in, boys,' I said, stepping back into the room and letting them in. 'What's the problem? What can I do for you?'

'Our television is broken,' said Pietro solemnly, exchanging a quick glance with his brother, who I suspected spoke only minimal English. 'It cannot be repaired until tomorrow and our favourite programme is being shown this afternoon. We are very sorry to inconvenience you, but may we watch it on your television?'

The decision didn't take much making.

'Yeah, sure. Be my guests,' I said, gesturing towards the TV and the settee I usually viewed from. 'I've got a visitor coming this evening but you're welcome to stay till then.'

'*Grazie! Grazie tanto!* Thank you so much!' This was Pietro again, the one who talked. I thought he was going to grab hold of me and hug me, and I was really looking forward to it . . . But he didn't. The brothers just settled themselves on the settee and switched on the TV, both wreathed in smiles. Pietro took the handset and began knowledgeably flicking buttons, and Paulo hunched forward, his elbows on his knees, his cute dimpled chin resting lightly on his fists, and his eyes already riveted on the screen.

'I'll just get some clothes on and then I'll come and watch with you,' I said, fully aware that I was simpering. They really were quite spectacular close up and the prospect of having them to myself for a couple of hours was intoxicating. 'What's on by the way?'

' "Football Italia"'!' they announced in unison. I just smiled and scooted for the bedroom before my face dropped again. An afternoon of football must be most women's nightmare, and this particular woman was no exception!

I'd been vaguely aware of the Italian soccer coverage on Channel Four, but of course I'd never watched it. That was going to change now, though, and grumbling to myself, I pulled on a scruffy old T-shirt, a pair of panties, and my dilapidated denim cut-offs. As I fluffed out my still-damp hair, I wondered whether I ought to put something better on, but it hardly seemed worth the effort. I looked quite fetching in my skimpy shorts and T-shirt, with my blonde locks all wild and shaggy. But Italian football fans were notoriously the most single-minded in Europe. You could barely get a word out of an English fan when there was a match on the telly, so these lads probably wouldn't even notice I

164

was in the room, no matter how sexily dressed I was.

Sure enough, they barely looked round when I sidled through the lounge towards the kitchen. Charming! I thought, preparing to start crashing things around to express my displeasure. But just then the younger one, Paulo, the non-English speaker, turned from what seemed to be a pretty crucial sweep down the right wing by the team in red and black, and gave me a smile of such dark-eyed warmth and sweetness that the pit of my belly turned to melted honey and suddenly the *calcio* didn't seem quite such a tedious sport after all.

'I'll just get us a drink, shall I?' I stammered, standing there like a lemon.

'*Grazie*,' he whispered, his brown eyes simmering briefly across my not-too-well-covered body before he returned his attention to the screen.

With Ollie in the doldrums, I'd laid in a good stock of wine, so I could easily spare a bottle for my Italians. But to only offer wine suddenly seemed a bit nigardly, so in the interest of Anglo-European relations, I had a rummage amongst all the extra food I'd stocked up with, and flung together a by-my-standards fairly impressive selection of *antipasti*.

Their praise was profuse as I put the tray down on the coffee-table, although I did notice them edging around me slightly so they could still see the screen while they thanked me.

'Thank you so much, Signorina Foxton,' said Pietro warmly. 'You should not have gone to all this trouble. We are already in your debt for permitting us to watch our programme.'

'My name's Georgina,' I answered, knocked sideways by the genuine beauty of his smile, 'but you can call me "Georgie", if you like.'

'*Grazie tanto*, Georgie,' he murmured, turning up the voltage on that grin.

Paulo backed up his brother with a stream of melodic, husky and quite spine-tingling Italian that made not one iota of sense to me, but turned my knees to jelly and made my sex quiver like one. God, these two were so gorgeous they were edible! It was a pity that I'd have to either score a goal or lie down naked in the penalty box to get them to notice me.

Having said that, a curious thing happened when I came to sit down. In what looked suspiciously like a set piece manoeuvre, Paulo scooted to one end of the sofa, and Pietro slid to the other. I sank down in the middle with an Italian striker on each wing. It was the old *uno due*, no less. I wondered if they'd take their eyes off the action long enough to notice how hard and erect my nipples were looking through the thin white cotton of my T-shirt . . .

It didn't seem so. When the wine was poured, and the olives and such handed round, all attention returned to the football. Even mine. Almost before I realised, I was actually following the game and rooting for the team in red and black shirts – Milan, Pietro informed me with pride. I vaguely remembered a neighbour saying that was where the boys were from, and that they'd come over to England to help their uncle set up a new restaurant. Now I'd got a team to support, I decided that AC Milan played very 'attractively', and the sight of those darkly powerful athletes, storming across the pitch, only served to remind me of the two equally dark and powerful males I had on either side of me. Slightly closer on either side of me, perhaps, than they had been originally.

Things came to a head when 'our' centre forward

scored a brilliant goal; rocketing one just past the fingertips of the keeper and putting Milan unassailably in the lead. As the ball crossed the line, both the brothers shrieked *'Forza Milano!'* then turned as one to kiss me. Two sets of Italian lips pressed hot and hard against my cheeks, two sets of Italian arms went around me to hug both me and the other brother – and the glass of wine I'd been sipping at the time was up-ended all over my front. I'd only just topped it up.

I was soaked. Thin white cotton clung like a second skin to my breasts, and if the brothers hadn't noticed my nipples before, there was no way they could avoid them now.

'Mi scusi!'

'Mi scusi!' they choroused, but as I turned from one golden-olive face to the other, I slowly, then rather quickly realised that they already had another national passion on their minds. A passion that flowed as hot in their veins as the football did . . .

In another effortless one-two they moved in on me. Pietro took the glass from my nerveless fingers, then eased the hem of my sodden T-shirt out of my shorts' waistband and pulled it up and over my head. Like an obedient puppet, I raised my arms to help him, and even as I did so, I felt Paulo working on first the button, then the zip of my shorts.

Half-heartedly I tried to protest, but Pietro slid an arm around my naked back and pulled me in close for a kiss. As his wine-scented tongue expertly prised open my mouth, I felt his free hand cup my right breast. His thumb skated delicately across my nipple, and as it did, his brother slid my shorts down over my hips and took my tiny lace panties off with them.

They'd stripped me. Just like that. And all I'd

done was let them . . . As his tongue went darting around my mouth, Pietro's fingers played havoc with my breasts. First one, then the other; squeezing, gently rolling the flesh, taking a nipple in his finger and thumb and devilishly rolling that too. The lovely sensations made my pelvis start pumping in sympathy. But those lower zones were now Paulo's special province . . .

'Bellissima,' he murmured, sliding a hand beneath my bottom and insolently stroking my cheeks. I felt his fingers splay, and one – the middle one – settle right in the crease and tickle the tiny hole there. His other hand surged into the attack from the front, his fingers combing my wiry curls to get at the treasures within.

With my breasts being tenderly mauled and my anus wickedly fingered, my clitoris woke up and said 'touch me' . . . In seconds I was slippery, aching and ready.

But my Italians were devils: diavoli; masters of choreographed teasing. With accuracy and artistry, my labia were slowly eased apart and the bud of my sex exposed. But not touched . . .

'Please,' I gasped as Pietro released my mouth and attached his lips to my neck.

'Patience, mi cara,' he whispered against my skin, nibbling his way to my collar bone as his fingers worked ceaselessly on my teats. My own hands rose from where they'd been limply lying beside me and I touched each man on his thigh. Then, without thought or hesitation, slid my fingers lower and covered their denim-covered crotches . . .

They were both solidly erect, the heat of their flesh quite distinct through the fabric of their jeans. I shuddered as I lay there between them; my hands on their sexes, their hands not on mine. Both these beautiful creatures would need satisfying soon, but how would I accomplish it? Take them one after the other? Together? I shuddered again – violently – and as Paulo's fingers moved naughtily in my bottom groove, his free hand circled slowly on my belly.

'*Che bella ragazza,*' he whispered, leaning in towards me, his body brushing his brother's as he took the mouth that Pietro had abandoned.

Paulo's tongue was less assertive than his sibling's but just as beguiling; it stroked lightly but surely against my own tongue as his fingers rode the furrow of my bottom.

I was wriggling now, shifting uneasily. They were stimulating my mouth, my breasts and my arse, but the core of my sex was still screaming.

It didn't have to scream for too long . . .

Somehow, I don't really know how, the brothers seemed to swarm all over me. As Paulo's tongue flicked insistently at mine, his brother's mouth cruised down to my nipple. Chuntering with satisfaction, he drew on it heavily, his fingers playing with the other peak and tweaking it to the rhythm of his sucks.

The pleasure in my breasts was fast turning to agony in my crotch, but gentle young Paulo had mercy. He wiggled a finger through my pubes and settled it with perfect precision on my clit. As he pressed lightly there and his other hand palpated my anus, I felt as if a circuit had completed inside me: nipples, clitoris, mouth, bottom. Every sensitive area was covered and attacked, and I came, grunting obscenely around Paulo's probing tongue. I seemed to climax for a long long time; more completely and beautifully than I had for ages. I was still throbbing when the brothers disengaged both their fingers and their mouths and after a whispered consultation in their own language, lifted me bodily from the couch and lowered me on to the rug.

Eyes closed, I just lay there. I knew I had a silly cat-with-the-cream grin on my face, but it didn't seem to matter one bit. My sex felt too hot, too wet and too glowing for me to worry about anything. I heard the brothers moving about nearby, and furniture being moved to make space. As the football commentator still enthused in the background, I heard the rustle of clothing and soft words muttered in Italian. Somebody had just scored when the sound from the television went quieter.

My clitoris and nipples tingled. The brothers were closing in on me again, and this time there would be no Italian football to distract their attention. I opened my eyes and looked towards them . . .

They were magnificent, classical, and superbly male; so different yet so similar. They both had silky Mediterranean tans and soot-black body hair that matched the hair on their heads, but in other ways there were delightful distinctions. Paulo was compact, heavily muscular without being gross, and had a cock that reflected his physique. Jutting out proudly, it was thick and stubby with a tip that was swollen and tempting. Pietro was longer and leaner – everywhere. His body looked slim and flexible and so did his cock. Its shape was narrow and elegant, but its length was breathtaking. He would reach inside me, go deeper than deep, find and touch my soul. And I wanted that so much.

As one, they sank down on to the rug and arranged themselves: Paulo at my side, Pietro between my outflung thighs. Both then carefully lifted me. Pietro raised my buttocks and presented the tip of his cock to my entrance, while Paulo slid an arm beneath my shoulders and twisted my upper body towards his temptingly out-thrust organ. As he rose up slightly on his knees and cradled the back of my head, he pulled cushions from the settee and piled them up beneath me for my comfort.

'Per favore,' he whispered, resting his glans against my lips like a sacrament.

'Per favore,' I heard from somewhere beyond him, just as Pietro pushed tentatively forward . . .

'Oh, yes! Please! Sì!' I cried, craning upwards to take Paulo in my mouth while my hips bucked hard against Pietro. Co-ordinating without words, both men surged into me and began to thrust.

Paulo was as careful and gentle as he'd been in everything so far, but it was definitely *him* fucking my mouth rather than *me* sucking his cock . . . And Pietro went in just as deep as I'd known and hoped he would. I was locked between them, my body jerking to their immaculate synchronised rhythm as my hands roved blindly over all the hot sleek Italian flesh I could reach.

Not that *their* hands weren't busy . . . A finger, I don't know whose, slid into my slit and rubbed me gently, while other fingers tightened on my nipples. I was pinched and pulled and jiggled and fondled . . . and all in time to the long hard strokes of Pietro's gliding cock.

I wanted to scream with joy but I was gagged by Paulo's thick rod. The sound, caged inside me, seemed to turn back on itself and explode in my sex as pleasure. My vagina clamped hard around Pietro, and my mouth went slack and loose and let in his brother still deeper.

It was too intense to last. The boys were too excited; their cocks too quivering, too bursting, too ready. And I was too full of heat and orgasm and pure, simple love to be able to bear it much longer.

They both cried out as they climaxed. Through a haze and from an enormous distance, I heard 'Gesúmaria!' and 'Ah! Dio mio!' I couldn't tell which religious exhortation was whose and I didn't care. I felt like praising heaven myself, but I couldn't. I just gulped and gobbled and wept, swallowing warm salty semen and coming like a storm around the cock that was pulsing inside me.

The next coherent thought I had was to notice that the football was over. There was a documentary of some kind on now, probably a very good one, but I was too blissed out and bleary-eyed to make sense of it. Unwinding myself from a tangle of sweaty limbs, I got up, switched off the set and padded away to the bathroom.

When I returned, by way of the kitchen and the fridge, the brothers were still dozing. Two sets of brown eyes fluttered open and two soft mouths smiled when I set down a fresh bottle of wine on the coffee table. Pietro sat up and reached out for me, but as he did, the doorbell rang and both he and his brother pulled faces of eloquent, little-boyish disappointment.

As I shrugged apologetically and turned towards the door, I thought about who I was expecting . . . Then I thought about my two handsome *tifosi* – and everything slotted neatly into place. I didn't even have to bother putting my clothes on this time . . .

Stepping back, I ushered Ollie through, and every mouth in the room – except mine – dropped open. Pietro and Paulo's because they must've thought they were seeing double; and Olivia's because her twin sister – me! – wasn't wearing a single stitch of clothing . . . and neither were the two Botticelli angels sitting on her rug!

'Ollie, meet Pietro and Paulo,' I said, hoping against hope I hadn't misjudged things. 'They came down to watch the football.'

The boys got gracefully to their feet, and I had to stifle my giggles. It was obvious that they were *extremely* pleased to meet my sister.

'Boys, this's my sister Olivia. She's come to stay with me for a few days.'

The brothers both smiled charmingly at Ollie, their open, ingenuous faces every so slightly at odds with the stiff erections that were pointing out boldly from their loins.

Would Ollie approve though? To my mind these two beautiful kindly Italians were just what she needed to help her forget her failed love affair. But there was every chance she might never want to see a man again.

I needn't have worried . . .

'Football fans, eh?' she said with a chuckle. 'Well, it certainly looks like somebody's scored here today!'

Dropping her case, she walked beside me to the rug and the boys, then glanced at the evidence of our 'match'.

'I do have to hand it to you, Georgie . . . Food, wine, *and* naked men! You really know how to cheer a girl up.'

And I had to hand it to the brothers. Ollie was as much a shock to them as they were to her, but even so their teamwork was as faultless as ever. One after the other they courteously kissed her hand, then with a swift nod to Paulo in my direction, Pietro kissed her full on the lips. He was just sliding the shirt from her shoulders as Paulo bore *me* down on to the rug. I smiled and curled my fist around his cock.

Moments later, as Paulo nudged open my labia and entered me, I heard a soft moan of pleasure and looked across to where Pietro was just easing into Ollie. Her pale legs wrapped around him in welcome and when his tight brown bottom began rising and falling, she cried out once again, and louder.

I turned away then, respecting my sister's privacy, and as Paulo starting moving too, I added my own happy cries to the mêlée.

Now, I've always babbled nonsense during lovemaking and this time was no exception. I was noisy; I was incoherent; and I was mindless. But I've got not one, not two, but *three* other people who'll swear I shouted '*FORZA ITALIA!*' as I climaxed!

Stranger than . . .

OOOOOOOH!

Elliot Witter nearly choked on his drink when a slim hand settled lightly on his penis. It was a woman's hand, gloved in leather, and its touch was both devilish and skilful. He felt the grain of the hide kiss the grain of his fine-textured genital skin and a fingertip trace his frenum. He sighed, sadly, and placed his glass back on the bar. It was such a shame that the hand existed only in his mind . . .

Elliot had always had a vivid imagiation, but for the last four weeks, three days and two and a half hours it'd been going bananas. Four weeks, three days and two and a half hours was the exact amount of time since he'd walked into the La Terrazza bar and fallen deep into his very first full-blown erotic obsession.

He'd only gone into the place out of curiosity. He'd been working late and felt stressed out, pissed off and bored with his relatively mundane existence. La Terrazza was a notorious sexual stomping ground, and as a young man whose turn to stomp was long overdue, he'd arrived with high hopes, a genuine thirst, and the beginnings of a very nice hard-on. He'd expected glitzy people, pricey drinks and plush, slightly pervy surroundings; what he hadn't expected was 'The Weirdo' . . .

He called her 'The Weirdo' because by most conventional standards of femininity, she was one. She was also the purest piece of sex he'd ever set eyes on, and when he'd first spotted her, perched languidly on a stool at the other end of the bar, he'd felt an instant turbulence in his trousers.

It shouldn't have happened. Before that moment, he'd liked soft and pretty girls – gentle, pliant little creatures with masses of candyfloss curls and sweet cuddly bodies to match.

But 'The Weirdo' didn't have any of these attributes. In fact there was nothing soft about her at all; she was a hard bitch, and her beauty was brittle and peculiar. Sleek, bright, gel-coated hair matched a sleek, bright decadent image; and though her body was just about as womanly as it was possible to be, she dressed it as if it were a man's.

Elliot knew who she was, of course. On the first night she'd already looked vaguely familir, and on the second, he'd asked the barman about her. It hadn't surprised him at all that she was the famous erotic novelist Diamanda; in fact he couldn't understand why he hadn't recognised her immediately. He had her photograph at home on the back of several book-jackets.

His goddess was as famous for her hedonistic, rule-breaking lifestyle as she was for her passionately purple prose: it was well-known in this city and in others that she liked lovers of either sex and often in multiple quantities.

Elliot would've died for just an instant of her attention, and for four weeks now, he'd seen those silky, painted lips in every one of his dreams, and those glinting, slanted eyes on every woman's face he encountered. Two days ago, she'd turned up wearing a pair of the finest of black leather gloves . . . and now, every time his guard went down, he kept feeling their touch on his cock.

The most frustrating thing about all this was that not once had she appeared to notice him. Whether alone or with a flutter of flamboyant friends, his Weirdo seemed to have all the company she required. Elliot had run a million inner scenarios of how their first meeting would go, but when it came to making them real, he was terrified she'd regard him with disdain; or worse still, pity.

Elliot's big problem was shyness. When women got to know him they usually rather liked him; he was no fool, he had a good job for someone of his relative lack of years, and though somewhat fragile-looking for a man, he was moderately handsome in a quiet way. But it was the 'getting to know' stage that was so fraught with difficulty. When faced with a pretty woman, his subtle intelligence deserted him and his pleasant looks turned a furious beetroot red. He'd blush and stammer and he'd know that even though a girl was trying to be kind, inside she was already planning her getaway.

In his dreams, though, he was a tiger. And in the dreams of these last four weeks, with the weird and wonderful Diamanda, he'd stood up on his hindlegs and roared!

He'd walk up to her at the bar, bold as brass and without a microsecond's hesitation. She'd smile that oblique red-lipped smile of hers and indicate immediately that he join her. They'd share a cocktail, or perhaps some suitably 'hard' drink like Scotch, no-ice no-water, then after about five minutes of his brilliant conversation, she'd tell him she just couldn't wait any more and that she had a suite reserved for them in a nearby hotel.

In a luxurious cream and gold rococo decorated bedroom, she'd divest herself of her severe, man-tailored clothing and reveal herself to be all breasts and voluptuous womanhood beneath. This part he knew to be true, because one night last week she'd shucked off her snazzy designer jacket in the warm, crowded bar, and the shirt underneath had been truly sensational. Classically styled but made from the sheerest and most gauzelike voile, it'd almost made Elliot faint. He – and everyone else in the room – had had a clear sight of her unfettered bra-less breasts. Twin, rounded orbs, high but plump, and with nipples that stood out like thick brown buttons . . .

Back in his dreams, he'd caressed these luscious mammaries with no further ado. She'd sobbed as he mounded and squeezed them, all her hardness turned to miraculous malleable softness, and wetness, and wantonness; for him . . .

'Yes! Oh, Elliot, yes!' was her scream as he first touched her, then entered her. No foreplay was required in this ecstatic world of perfection, and penetration was effected in a single snag-free glide.

Tumbling back to reality, and almost falling off his stool in the process, Elliot sighed with regret. He really loved the 'hotel room' fantasy, although he had to admit it wasn't entirely all his own work. The protagonists – Diamanda and himself – were his choice of course, but the scenario, the setting and the nitty-gritty of the bedroom action came straight from one of the lady's own stories, *The Spider's Web*, which was all about a beautiful, sexually voracious woman who picked up young men in bars and lured

178

them to hotel rooms to fuck them.

Would that it would happen for real, thought Elliot desperately as he considered ordering another drink. It didn't look as if she was coming in tonight.

Two small beers later, he felt the urge to visit the men's room and as he trudged wearily in its direction, he decided that once he'd dealt with his natural function, he'd cut his losses and leave. When Diamanda wasn't in La Terrazza, its crowds of laughing glitterati served only to remind him how lonely he was.

When he returned, he took one last hopeful look around . . . and suddenly every nerve-end in his body went 'yow!' – especially the ones in his cock.

Right in the far corner the room, discreetly tucked away, with a large video jukebox. And standing in front of it – headphones atop her gel-polished hair, and her whole body weaving to the unheard beat – was Diamanda. Alone for the moment, and wearing what seemed to be a leather teddy-boy suit – draped jacket and tight-cut trousers – she was studying the screen before her with an expression of unalloyed enjoyment.

Elliot's heart started to pound like a steamhammer in his chest. She looked so bizarre in her pervy leather suit, but lost in the music she seemed – paradoxically – ten times more approachable.

As he reached her, Diamanda glanced away from the screen, smiled, and before he'd time to open his mouth, looked him disconcertingly straight in the eye.

'I –' Elliot began, but she silenced him with a finger to her glazed lips and mimed that he should wait until the track was over. It was arrogant, and quite typical of what he'd imagined of her, but like a helpless slave, he obeyed.

179

Up close, her straight-nosed profile was so fine and pure it almost hurt his eyes; and her bodyscents – both natural and artificial – were so potent they made him giddy. It was like standing next to a myth, an illusion, a chimera; and when the number finished Elliot gasped with relief. It felt like ten minutes since he'd taken a breath!

As she drew the lightweight headphones off and hooked them on the side of the machine, Elliot was gripped by panic. He *had* to speak first. If he just stood here gawking like a loon, she'd think him pathetic and the idea of that was almost physically painful.

'I've been watching you,' he said, nervous but surprised by the strength and apparent calm of his own young voice . . . then even more surprised by the effect it had on Diamanda.

She was shocked; astounded; flabbergasted. It was as simple as that. Elliot couldn't figure out what was so radical about the four ordinary words he'd uttered, so he repeated them.

'I've been watching you,' he said again, 'I hope you don't mind.'

Surprise seemed to soften that pale, sharp face somehow, mute it into something far less intimidating. She looked almost mellow when she answered. 'Now how the jiggery did I know you were going to say that, I wonder? It's uncanny.'

He didn't know what on earth she was on about, but her voice locked him under her spell. It was light, melodic and faintly affected. In a man it would've sounded camp, and even in a woman the timbre was decidedly weird; but to Elliot it seemed as if every syllable was a gobbet of warmed honey that trickled down his spine and flowed into a pool around his balls. His prick stiffened immediately

180

and formed an aching insistent bar that pushed at the fabric of his trousers. Without thinking, he looked down at the obvious bulge; and to his horror, Diamanda's eyes followed his.

'Oh, wow,' she breathed, 'This gets weirder and weirder.'

'I'm sorry. You don't know me. This's so embarrassing,' he burbled, feeling the blush come racing up his throat and his erection get horrifically harder.

'Don't worry about it,' Diamanda answered airily, her initial surprised reaction melting into something more teasing and confident; a kind of amused resignation that was still ever-so-slightly laced with wonder. 'And I *do* know you – in a way. You're not the only person who watches people . . . I do it all the time. How do you think I get ideas for my books and stories?' She paused, touched a long lacquer-tipped finger to her chin, and seemed, still, to be slightly taken aback, 'Although it doesn't usually work out like this. I must be turning into a seer in my old age.'

A what? thought Elliot, feeling out of his depth and enthralled. 'I've got all your books,' he gasped in a vain attempt to bring some normality to their discourse. 'I think they're great! So well written . . . So real.' Oh Lord, he was only getting in deeper. She'd think him a toadying fool now, as well as a sexfreak with no control of his willy!

But all she did was shake her head and smile. 'You sweet, sweet thing,' she murmured, looking down at his betrayingly tented trousers. 'Look, would you like me to do something about that? I don't usually plunge in quite so precipitiously, but after what you said and all . . . I simply don't think I can resist!'

But being propositioned like this, in a public place, quite literally struck him dumb. All the more so because she still seemed to be talking in riddles.

'We could go somewhere right now—' She paused and glanced at her heavy man's watch as if making an appointment to discuss the trade figures, 'Oh shit! I've to meet somebody else and I don't think I've time . . . Just let me check.'

As Elliot looked on, astounded and yet deeply titillated by the sheer outrageousness of it all, Diamanda fished into one of her jacket pockets and rummaged around. The first item she drew out was a book, which she passed to Elliot, muttering 'Hold this!' as she dove in for another search.

Taking the book, he realised it was a thinnish volume, in mint condition, and had Diamanda's own picture on the back.

Good God, it was her latest novel! One he hadn't read but was dying to. It wasn't even due out till next month. He studied the title – *Watching Me, Watching You* – then carefully flipped it open.

Words leapt up from the page at him. Words that in his current hyper-sensitised state, carried arousing and magical weight: 'naked', 'moist', 'distended'. Every letter, every sound in his head, every nuance of meaning seemed to scream to his cock about the body of the writer herself.

'You can borrow that if you like,' Diamanda said, looking up briefly from the wafer-thin portable computer notepad she'd pulled out of her other pocket.

'Er . . . Thanks.' He closed the book, not daring to read further. The prose was inflammatory to say the least, at a moment when his senses were burning already.

One of the strangest, most compelling women

he'd ever met was consulting an electronic diary to see if she could fit him in for a sexual quickie! It seemed about as likely as one of his masturbatory fantasies, and yet it was happening.

'Oh dear, what an absolute drag,' she muttered, flipping off the tiny microcomputer, 'I've to be out of here in half an hour. And tomorrow I'm off to the South of France to research my next novel.' She slid the gadget back in her pocket, and reached out to touch his face. 'We could be hot together, you and I. I just know it!' Her hand dropped to his, took the book, then slid it into his pocket, 'You can read that later, my sweet. When I've gone . . .' She took his empty hand, drew it to her mouth and kissed it moistly, running his tongue over his empty palm. Elliot knew now he could die a happy man. 'Come on! We haven't much time but we can still have some fun!'

With a determined tug on the hand she'd just kissed, she urged him into motion, and led him quickly across the room, her eyes bright and glittering and her fine mouth curved in the most wicked grin he'd ever seen in his life!

Fun? Oh Lord, yes! Thirty-five minutes later his knees were still shaking! It'd been like being back at school; being far too young again; doing naughty things in cramped and uncomfortable places – and loving every second of it! Somehow they'd found themselves in a tiny cubicle in the men's room with their trousers around their ankles and their hands at work on each other's crotches.

He'd tried to protest, but there was no saying no saying 'no' to Diamanda. After only the most cursory of 'reccies', she'd dragged him in, pushed him into the first open stall and bolted the door. Just as she was unzipping her sleazy leather trousers, there was the sound of voices just outside. Lots of them!

'Stay cool,' she'd mimed, pulling her thin and strangely plain white panties down to her knees and leaving them there, stretched, as she took his hand where he could feel her moist readiness. 'Do me!' she breathed, positioning his finger on her clitoris.

He started to rub instinctively, his finger sliding on the big hard bud, then missed as beat as her hands attacked his belt. She bobbed her pelvis at him impatiently, and he managed to re-establish his rhythm, in spite of the fact she was pushing down *his* clothing by now. When his trousers were pooled around his ankles, she moved temporarily off his hand and pushed his briefs out of the way too. When they were scrunched somewhere around calf level, she took his right hand again and crammed his shaking fingers into her slit, then left him to it and took a firm but measured hold on his erection.

In spite of the nearness of other lavatory users, he couldn't suppress his broken gasp.

'Shut up,' mouthed Diamanda, her eyes wild and her own breathing breaking up as she pumped her loins on his hand.

Her fingers were merciless. Working his prick on long smooth strokes, she slid the skin deftly over the inner blood-stiffened pole with – every so often – subtle lateral swivel that was so amazing it almost blew his ears off. Jerking and squirming, he cracked his tossing head on the cubicle wall, and Diamanda laughed soundlessly and re-doubled her digital onslaught. Elliot fought for breath, and wriggled helplessly against the thin barrier that divided them from the unknown men outside.

'What you doin' in there, you faggots?' called out

a gleeful voice.

As Diamanda opened her mouth to answer, with a reaction speed he wouldn't have thought possible under the circumstances, Elliot wrenched his hand from her pulsing sex and clapped it across her lips. Her sculpted eyebrows waggled at him as he felt her licking her own juices off his hand.

'Behave!' he mimed frantically as she nipped at the soft flesh of his palm and began a slow remorseless squeeze of his cock.

'Keep your tongues out, boys!' called the voice again, surprisingly amiably. Elliot bit hard on his lip as the squeezes below turned to a furious milking action. His whole body seemed on the point of explosion as he listened to pissing and washing and general sprucing up sounds ... then at last, footsteps, a slamming door and silence.

'You crazy bitch!' he hissed, releasing Diamanda's mouth. Her lipstick was slightly smudged at one corner; it was the first time he'd ever seen her less than immaculate. 'What the hell are you trying to do? Get us arrested?' he gasped, as she grinned and licked her smeary lips.

'I'm trying to get us off!' she drawled, then before he could do anything about it, she was on her knees, sucking his distended tool into her mouth.

As her tongue worked him, Elliot was aware, principally, of two sensations. One was the cold cubicle wall, so slick and smooth against his working bottom. The other was a great ball of swirling heat and wetness that enclosed his quivering prick.

Diamanda's mouthwork was superb. She seemed to have the ability to create a hard pulling vacuum around him, whilst beating furiously with her tongue on the most susceptible areas of his penis. In

185

moments the semen that'd been suppressed with so much difficulty came spurting out with the most perfect of ease. Elliot grunted freely as each pulse of spunk brought a heavy throb of pleasure with it, a vibration down the entire rigid length of his enclosed and well-sucked prick. If a dozen city policemen had bashed down the door at that very moment, he couldn't have cared less.

Afterwards, he knelt before Diamanda and licked her to a climax she expressed only by the vicious pulling of his hair and the involuntary spasming of her flesh beneath her tongue. More patrons milled about outside as she came, and it was several minutes before the coast was clear and the two of them were able to zip up and sneak out of the cubicle. Even then, and in spite of Elliot's protests, Diamanda insisted on spending several long minutes in front of the mirror repairing her ravaged lipstick. She laughed merrily when he urged her to hurry up because it was, after all, the *men's* room she was preening in!

With her lipstick restored to a gleaming bow, she wouldn't kiss him *au revoir* either, though she did give him an affectionate squeeze of the crotch as she bade him farewell – much to the amusement of several men entering the cloakroom that they'd just left.

'We'll finish this when I get back from France, shall we?' she said as they walked back towards the bar. 'I'll phone you. We'll do Chapter Two then!' She gave him that strange, faintly befuddled look again then, and shook her head. 'Good grief, boy, I don't even know your name!'

'It's Elliot Witter,' he whispered, then tagged on his telephoned number for luck.

'I thank you for that, young Elliot,' she said

186

archly, whipping out her notepad and recording his 'particulars'. 'And for everything else too. I'll be in touch!'

With that, she'd swept away, leaving Elliot with a wrung-out mind, a wrung-out cock and a pre-publication copy of a racy new novel still stuffed in his jacket pocket.

A few minutes later, he was sitting at the bar with a fresh beer before him which her lingering flavour on his lips made him reluctant to lift up and drink. With the vague feeling that he'd spent the last half hour in a 'trip' at least twice as exotic as its contents, he took out the pristine, unhandled book and thumbed it open at page one. As he began to read, his hands shook, his flushed face drained to dead white, and his penis – unbelievably – swelled up to a new and even harder and more aching erection . . . Was truth stranger than fiction? Or were the two about as weird as each other?

The woman was as unusual as she was beautiful, the first line read, *and as the young man drew close, he felt his flesh grow stiff in his pants. He had to speak – it was now or never . . .*

'I've been watching you,' he told her, his voice nervous but strong . . .

The Man in Black

FUNNY THINGS CAN happen when you're bored, they say . . . And one afternoon last summer, in a large Birmingham hotel, boy was I bored!

The lecture was 'Maximising your Selling Potential through Eye Contact' and the only thing my eyes wanted contact with was the inside of my eyelids. The speaker was short and tubby and dressed in Top Man meets *Miami Vice*. For my part, he'd no potential whatsoever . . . The seminar delegates weren't much better: the men were a bunch of yuppie pseuds and the women – with the single exception of a northern lass I'd teamed up with – were hard-faced chainstore power-dressers who'd do a damn sight more than make eyes to get a sale.

Yeah, the selling game was just a great big con, and as soon as this lot was over, I was out of it! This particular lecture was the pits interest-wise, and I'd already tried the usual distractions. I'd counted the pin-stripes on the wimpish back in front of me. I'd drawn seven different doodles on my blank notepad. I'd priced the outfit of the girl sitting next to the wimp. Judy, my Yorkshire mate, was as fed up as I was, but when we'd exchanged commiserations, we'd been furiously shushed by the dedicated types around us. Good God, were they really believing this shit?

After twenty minutes, I'd completely had it. Unbuttoning my jacket, I mussed up my hair and crossed and recrossed my nylon-clad thighs. If I couldn't find a diversion, I'd create one! The plan was to upset all the males on my row, and make it as difficult for them to concentrate as it was for me. I'm not a raving beauty, I admit, but with long, shapely legs, tousled red hair and a very decent pair of breasts, I always get second looks. But today, I wasn't even getting first ones. And especially not from—

Then I saw him. I saw him and I couldn't figure out why I hadn't seen him before . . . Leaning against the wall at the end of my row, was a man dressed all in black: the most gorgeous hunk I'd ever seen. Why he was leaning against the wall, and why he was wearing black denim in a room full of mock Armani? I never stopped to ask.

He appeared to be listening to the lecture, though why I really don't know. He looked less like a sales rep than I did.

He was just my type, though: medium height, slim, dark – very dark. There was black in him somewhere, or maybe Latin. Whatever it was, he'd a deep toffee-coloured tan, jet black hair, and big brown bedroom eyes. He was so perfect for me I could've designed him. He'd got that sexy, dodgy, almost girlish look that gets me every time . . . but with a crotch, in sprayed on jeans, that belonged to no girl I've ever known!

I just couldn't stop ogling it – I mean him! – and any second he was going to turn round and catch me . . .

But he didn't. He just stood and stared at the stage,

a solemn, almost sad expression on his smooth angelic face.

God, he was a turn on! I'd never fallen in lust this fast before. Or fallen this hard. The man in black reached everything instantaneously. My breasts ached, my heart pounded, and my sex became warm and moist. I was a pot that badly needed stirring.

As if he knew I was watching, he suddenly shifted in his sentinel pose. Flexing restlessly, he drew up one leg, flatted his foot to the wall and tapped it in time to some unheard beat. The denim stretched to destruction over his thighs and I thought I'd melt in my chair. His body was long, lean and whippy-looking. His face fine-featured but strong. He'd be fabulous in bed, I told myself. Graceful dynamite. Those narrow hips would pump like a jackhammer . . .

As I thought it I felt it! I swear I did! I was filled, stuffed, stretched. A bar of hard flesh moved inside me . . . I think I moaned – but I can't be sure – and in that moment, he turned towards me, and his face lit up with a beautiful, knowing, narrow-eyed smile – as if he really were on top of me and giving me his all!

'Are you all right, Jackie?' whispered a voice beside me, and I turned away from the man in black and his phantom prick and dragged myself back to reality.

Judy was studying me worriedly.

'You've gone all white, love,' she observed.

'It's okay, I'm fine!' I hissed back, ignoring the frowning faces around us. 'It's just a bit hot in here.'

I wasn't fine actually; but it would've been rather difficult to describe the problem discreetly. Nevertheless, Judy was a good soul and deserved a treat. I

190

wouldn't be selfish.

'What do you think of *him* then?' I said, nodding towards the end of the row. 'Dishy or what?'

'Who?' she replied, looking puzzled.

'*Him*, you dummy! The guy leaning against the wall!'

But when I turned back in his direction . . . the man in black had gone.

I soon had time to ponder this disappearance. The seminar was a lost cause as far as I was concerned, so I skipped the next lecture and went for a walk around the city. Judy, poor soul, had to make notes for her boss, or she'd have joined me.

I was supposed to be thinking about a new job, but ten seconds out of the hotel, I was dreaming about the man in black. How on earth had he got out of that hall so fast? I'd only looked away for seconds, and the exit was right at the back of the room. Why hadn't I seen him leave? I'd been so tuned into him . . .

The fact he'd been there at all was puzzling. He wasn't at the seminar because I'd have spotted him like a shot. Ditto if he'd been staff.

As I walked, I brooded over what might've been. I would've liked a chance to talk to him . . . Who was I kidding? I wanted to screw him! But a little conversation – between sessions – wouldn't have gone amiss.

I half hoped I'd get that peculiar sensation again while I walked. The ghost of his prick inside me. It didn't happen, but my inventive mind made up for it. By the time I got back to the hotel, we'd done everything I could think of, and a few I'd never thought of before!

Once in the foyer, I scanned around hopefully,

but there was no joy. No man in black to fulfil my lurid fantasies, or deal with their physical consequences. My panties were wet and my sex so inflamed I could hardly walk. If he'd appeared right then and there, I'd have fucked him on the spot!

No, that's exaggerating . . . but I'd have found a way to chat him up.

It dawned on me in the lift just how long I'd been out wandering. The lift was crammed. People were returning to their rooms to change for dinner, and it was hot in the crush of bodies. Leaning tiredly against the wall, I thought of my man in black leaning against his wall. My eyelids drooped and closed . . .

The hotel had nearly a dozen floors, and as I drowsed unnoticed I heard the lift doors swishing to and fro, and people getting out at their stops. The motion and the heat acted like a drug, and I was almost comatose when the lift jolted to a sudden, neck-wrenching halt. My eyes flew open. There – alone in the lift with me – stood the man in black.

'You!' I said stupidly, dazed by having him so, so close at last. He was too close now though. Suddenly I was scared – scared shitless – but just like before, I couldn't stop staring. Staring at a dark, silent figure who stared unblinkingly back at me.

At close range he was sensational: the face seraphic, solemn, and achingly sad, the body a black poem of sex. And I saw something else now . . .

His smooth brown throat was ringed with a scar: livid and fresh-looking, it was a necklace of pain that I longed to kiss and soothe. Irresistibly drawn, I trod the width of the lift and stood before him.

'I—'

It was all I managed. My voice died as the lights did, and we were plunged into utter blackness. All I could see were two flashing indicators: floors one and three blinking alternately. But before I could drawn breath to cry out, arms like iron bands whipped around me, and a strangely cool mouth crushed mine.

It was what I'd wanted, but in the terrifying darkness I struggled. For the first time, I heard his voice. 'No!' he cried, 'No! Don't leave me. Please don't leave me!'

The voice was a match for the face: beautiful – though obviously distressed – light-toned, yet disturbingly rich.

'It's all right,' I answered, gentling him as I'd always known I would. 'I won't leave you.'

It was a ludicrous thing to say, because neither of us was going anywhere. But I see now that there are others ways of leaving.

'Don't leave me!' he murmured, ignoring the fact I'd answered, 'She left me. She said I was too young, too naive; that I didn't know anything.'

He was so upset, so agonised, that it seemed the most natural thing in the world to pull him down to the floor and kiss and hold him as he'd kissed and held me.

'I shouldn't be here,' he muttered raggedly as I tugged open his shirt and licked blindly at the abrasive line of his scar. 'I should've moved on. But I can't go. I need you! I need you so much! Don't hurt me like she did.'

I'd no idea what he was talking about, but I didn't care. My fingers were already working on his belt, his zip, his briefs. Kisses weren't enough for my man in black. He needed the comfort only my body could give.

Delicately, I eased out his prick, and almost wept because I couldn't see it. He was more, far more

193

than I'd dreamed of: big, hard, and already slick with juice. Yet as I ran my fingers along his velvet shaft – then heard him moan as I lightly squeezed the tip – his flesh was quite cold to the touch. But it was a welcome coldness; a salve for the aching heat in my sex. He moaned again, then his hands were in my blouse and kneading my breasts as I struggled out of my lust-soaked pants.

Kicking them away, I lay back and let my thighs fall wide open. With a wordless mysterious grace, the man in black moved over me and pressed his cool prick to my gaping, liquid crevice. There was an uncouth grunt as he pushed it in, and to this day, I can't say whether it was him or me. I only know that having him in me was the most sublime experience of my life. That spectral fuck in the conference hall was nothing compared to this. He felt huge inside me, thrusting and plunging with a remorseless, measured power. Pounding me against the carpeted floor, he wept and whispered against my neck. The words were meaningless, but his tears, trickling on my skin, were what finally pushed me over . . .

All of a sudden I was dying. Falling, coming and flying through space . . . My body grabbed his in a spasm so immense and glorious it seemed to wrench my womb from its roots and send the whole length and breadth of my cunt up in flames. A scream tore from my throat, and twinned with his as we spun through the void in a long, hot, pumping convulsion that went on and on and on into oblivion . . .

'How do you feel, love?' asked Judy from a great distance, and suddenly I was looking up into her face, then seeing my hotel room behind her.

'What . . . What happened?' I mumbled. My

mouth dry and cotton-woolly, and when Judy held a glass to my lips, I slurped water thirstily. When she took it away, I tried to frame questions.

She beat me to it with an answer. 'Don't worry, love,' she said gently, 'you've had a fright but you're fine now.'

'But, Judy, I—'

'You were in the lift on your own and there was a power failure. It jammed between floors and you must've panicked and fainted.' She patted my hand reassuringly, 'you were only stuck for a few minutes, but being alone in the darkness must've freaked you out—'

'Alone! What do you mean . . . alone?'

'There was only you in the lift, love.' She eyed me worriedly. 'They brought you here when they got you out, and the hotel nurse checked you over. She said you were okay and I should let you sleep. That was last night.' She pointed in the direction of the partly drawn curtains. The morning sun was streaming through them.

'Alone?' I repeated numbly.

Judy looked puzzled, but she wasn't half as confused as me. I couldn't remember being carried to my room, or being examined by a nurse. But being flat on my back with the man in black between my legs was as clear as if it'd happened two seconds ago. I still felt sore! Nobody could tell me I'd been alone in that lift.

'You weren't the only drama here yesterday, you know.'

Judy was trying to distract me now. 'There was a suicide in the hotel.' She picked up a newspaper – a local morning edition that she must've been reading while I'd slept. Turning a few pages, she opened it.

'It seems there's been a famous actress staying

195

here, and she'd got a toyboy with her.' With a horrified fascination I watched her finger track along the print. 'Anyway, they had a massive row and she stormed off and left him; leaving the poor sod so upset he hung himself! In the shower! It's a crying shame. There's a picture of him: he was bloody gorgeous!'

She held out the paper to me, but suddenly I didn't want to see that 'bloody gorgeous' dead man.

'When did it happen?' My voice quavered. I didn't want to know.

'Yesterday afternoon, it says,' she said, dropping the paper into my lap, 'It doesn't bear thinking about, does it? While we were listening to all that crap about eye contact, this lovely bloke was choking to death.'

I shouldn't have looked.

But I did.

There, looking back at me, was the perfect, fine-boned face of my beautiful man in black . . .

A Pet for Christmas

THEY WEREN'T THE biggest he'd ever seen, but boy did they look firm!

Niall Christopher spread out his copy of *Penthouse* and gazed at the most gorgeous pair of breasts he'd ever seen. High and delicately rounded they went perfectly with the tiny waist, the long, sleek thighs and the petal-pink, sweetly-crinkled sex that peeped demurely yet raunchily through a bush of flossy gold-brown curls.

'Misty – our Mystery Yuletide Pet' the write-up announced, and as his hand slid to his prick – in homage to her beautiful, bountiful flesh – Niall couldn't think of anything he'd like for Christmas better. He'd only bought this mag today, but he was already head-over-heels in lust with pages fifty-two through fifty-nine!

And why not? He needed something to console him and marvellous Misty was keeping more than just his spirits up. Looking at her scrumptious body, he could forget what a crappy Christmas he was having. He could forget this godawful shitty cold he'd caught and – most of all – he could even forget

197

that imminent debacle of all debacles, he company's annual 'do'.

Agh! The 'do'. An event that was both a let-down and a cock-up in one fell swoop.

Things would've been so different if he'd been going with Selina. Or – and his prick leapt like a salmon at the thought – if mouthwatering Misty were his date for the night. As it was, instead of going to the party with the branch sexpot, he was going with the branch 'mouse'. Mary Marwood, a brown-haired, blue-stockinged systems analyst, was the firm's newcomer, and a right plain jane if ever there was one. Niall couldn't believe he'd gone and invited her.

Oh bugger! Oh bugger, bugger, bugger! The biggest bash of the year: a free booze-up at the firm's expense and an 'all-round ' night in a posh hotel. Squiring a stunning blond to the 'do' and then – down boy! – then giving her a seven-inch Christmas present in the room next door to his. Oh God, it should've been perfectamundo!

But now Selina had dumped him, and swapped rooms with mousy Miss Mary . . .

'She's not *that* bad, I suppose,' he philosophised mournfully to the beautiful but two dimensional nude in the his magazine, then poured himself a whisky from the bottle he'd bought – along with the *Penthouse* – to make his life more bearable, 'but I wish to God she was you, Misty, my angel!'

Funny though, he mused blearily, flicking through Misty's spread. The Mouse and the Pet were fundamentally the same animal: woman. So why couldn't Mary achieve the same effect? If she fluffed her hair out, like Misty's, instead of wearing that prim plait; if she wore hot, red lipstick, and clothes that showed her shape . . . Well, she might be halfway decent!

Misty's outfit was totally indecent, and in the big centrefold picture, it showed every last bit of her shape! Her heavy satin wrap rippled across the bed beneath her, its rich plum-purple folds a perfect foil for her creamy, opulent and otherwise stark naked body. Phooaargh! Niall's fingers stroked his hardened shaft as he catalogued her other accessories. A maroon diamanté-trimmed domino surrounded but didn't hide her brilliant electric blue eyes and a pair of sheer lace gloves in the same shade covered her dainty hands. Her right gloved forefinger was pressed saucily into her full red mouth, and her left one pointed artistically yet oh-so-rudely to yet *another* pair of glistening lips.

Mousy Mary had mud-brown eyes that she hid behind heavy unflattering spectacles, and Niall seriously wondered if she had a fanny at all! Yet those lack-lustre eyes had sparkled once today.

They'd been in the corridor, sorting their out bags, when this very magazine had slipped from his hold-all and fallen at Mary's feet. He'd blushed at a prime case of sod's law, and expected Mary to blush even redder at the sight of Misty in all her open-legged glory.

But Miss Mouse had just smiled: a strangely appealing smile in one so dull. 'What a beautiful girl,' she'd commented in her soft-spoken voice. 'Is this your type, Niall?'

For one horrid moment, he'd thought the Mouse was flirting, but then she'd picked up the magazine, folded it neatly, and handed it to him. Afterwards, Niall couldn't figure out for the life of him what'd made him invite her to the party.

But did he really have to go?

I'm far too ill to party, he decided, drinking long and deep of his whisky and rubbing absently at the staple in Misty's naughty navel. I'll stay here with you, my goddess, he told her, beginning to feel distinctly woozy. He'd not had all that much whisky, but obviously even the wee-est of drams was a bad idea on top of medication.

Yes, he felt extremely odd now, although not in a wholly unpleasant way. Perhaps it was the masked temptress beneath his fingers making him delirious with her lush naked body and the promise of sex so mind-blowing he'd probably never ever achieve it with a real woman?

He imagined plunging into that juicy pink furrow, caressing those high, fruity breasts, and gazing into those brilliant, almost unnaturally-blue eyes as he shafted her. In his mind he kissed her sticky red-painted mouth and fucked it with his tongue as he fucked her luscious clinging sex. Oh God, the works bash could go screw itself! The party was right here with Misty, and the stroke of his strong right hand.

He flipped open the brand new robe he'd bought to impress Selina and took hold of the tool he'd hoped would also impress her. This's for you, Misty my darling, he pledged, beginning a slow luxuriant masturbation and wishing he felt just a little more 'with it' to enjoy the process.

To hell with blondes and Christmas parties! It's just you and me, my pussy pet! We'll have a ball together. But reaching out for his drink – with the hand that wasn't clutching his plonker – he suddenly had a slightly deflating thought. As if on cue, there was a soft rap on his door.

Mousy Mary! Knocking back the drink – then regretting it as his head span wildly – Niall quickly fastened his robe and stumbled to let her in.

'Are you okay?' the dark, worried-eyed girl

enquired, and Niall could've wept at the difference between the fantasy of a second ago and the drab reality of now.

Yet, spaced-out as he was, he was forced to admit Mary *had* made an effort. Her brown hair was wound in a slightly softer sort of coil, and her fine complexion and regular features were graced with a subtle trace of make-up. Unfortunately, she still wore her gruesome glasses, and the rich fabric of her dress – a kind of burgundy satin that looked strangely familiar – was made up into a disappointingly pouchy shape.

'Thassa pretty dress . . .' Niall was shocked by the slur in his own voice, and even more upset when having stood up far too quickly he fell right down again!

'I'm not pissed, honestly!' he protested as Mary helped him into the armchair and laid a cool hand on his red-hot brow. 'I've got this stinking cold. I'm ill! I'm really, really ill!'

'Yes, of course you are.' Mary picked up the fallen *Penthouse*, and smiled – yet again – at the sight of Misty's beautiful wide-open fanny. What is it with her? Niall wondered through his haze. Is she a lezzie? Does *she* fancy Misty too?

'Is this your cure?' she enquired, shaking her head slowly and looking down at him with such a knowing and suddenly quite sexy look that he almost – in his befuddled state – started to fancy *her*!

'I . . . er . . . dunno,' he muttered, his eyelids drooping. Any minute now he'd probably pass out. 'Thassa a real pretty dress,' he repeated, guilty again at letting her down.

'It's my favourite colour,' she said evenly as she smoothed the hair back from his feverish brow, 'Look Niall, I think you should stay here and get some rest. You'll feel better after a sleep. You might even have a nice dream.'

Niall wasn't quite sure what she was on about: his brain seemed full of cotton wool, his body heavy and powerless. 'A nice dream,' he muttered, seeing the spectre of Misty's fantastic body as the blackness drifted down.

The next thing he heard was the slick of his room door closing. Disorientated, he scrubbed at his eyes, but when he opened them he realised the sound *wasn't* someone leaving but someone coming in. Thoughtful Miss Mouse had dimmed the lights, and in the gloom Niall could just make out a dark shape hovering by the door. A slim figure wearing something long and vaguely wine-coloured. Thank God! It was only Mary come back to check on him.

"S okay, Mary, I'm all right,' he called out, 'Don't waste your time on me. Get down to the party and have some fun.'

The figure seemed to sway slightly, although Niall couldn't be sure whether it was his visitor who moved so sinuously or a distortion created by his virus-fuddled brain . . .

'Mary?'

What the fuck was she doing? Suddenly Niall felt slightly rattled. 'Mary! Is that you?' he demanded fractiously – as the hidden one broke slowly from cover.

'Oh God! Oh God, oh God, oh God!' Niall licked his dry lips, and frozen in the act of getting up, he fell back in his chair like a nerveless doll.

Still swaying, but in the most erotic way he'd ever seen because her heels were five inches high, the yuletide Penthouse pet sashayed elegantly forward.

I'm hallucinating! thought Niall, deprived of what

little strength he had as his dream woman advanced upon him. He was paralysed; pinned. And as Misty reached his chair and stood before him in all her sensual magnificence, he recognised the exact same mask, gloves and wrap that she wore in the Christmas spread. All in that same rich vinous shade he'd ... he'd seen somewhere else this evening. Somewhere. He didn't know where.

'Misty,' he whispered, still locked in his seat.

The apparition didn't answer but just smiled archly, her gleaming red mouth parting in delicious temptation. What she did next made Niall's prick rise like an iron bar and his heart nearly burst in his chest.

In a smooth dream-like movement she parted her dark satin wrap and revealed the pale, utterly perfect body beneath. She was *Penthouse*-naked under the watery silk and her full, yet delicate shape was as a thousand times more stunning in the flesh than it was on the flat paper pages.

He could see every curve and hollow. The puckered peachy areolae of her peerlessly rounded breasts, every silky cream-white inch of her flawless skin. The achingly-sweet curve of her belly. The endearing yet salacious cluster of curls that shielded her fragrant vulva.

Boy, she was fragrant! Niall knew he wasn't imagining things now, because he could smell the pungent, unmistakeable smell of a highly aroused woman! The scent washed over him like a wave, filling his head with magic, his crotch with lust and his mouth with a great flood of saliva.

As if reading his addled mind, Misty shimmied like a dancer, then raised one long sleek-toned leg and placed her foot on the chair-arm just inches from his trembling prick. It was a lewd move yet divinely graceful, and Niall surrendered to unbearable temptation. Opening his robe, he exposed his sex as she'd exposed hers. He could see her fanny quite clearly now, and as her hips wafted slowly towards him, the woman-smell floated potently in his direction. The spittle pooled around his trembling tongue and he was forced to swallow.

He swallowed again as Misty tugged off one lace glove and tossed it away. Again, as she parted her labia with her still-belaced hand an started touching her clitoris with her long, slender and very naked right forefinger.

Niall grasped his cock and jerked it furiously in time to his dream-girl's masturbation. Misty's finger moved faster and faster, rubbing her clit with manic intensity.

She paused only once in her wild race towards climax . . .

Though she still spoke not a word, the flood of juice between her legs was soon so profuse it was audible. Scooping up a shining fingerful, she took it to her panting lipsticked mouth and slurped it with a crude, almost caricatured relish. Then, before Niall could even breath, much less speak, she repeated the vulgar gesture and pushed the results into his mouth.

Her taste was salt, musk and a sea-like richness. Niall moaned out loud at its pure deliciousness and leaned forward hungrily for more. Only to have it denied, and almost weep with frustration as Misty resumed her frantic rubbing.

Within seconds her hips were bucking in an obscene, pumping frenzy, and her beautiful face was distorted – what Niall could see of it – in an animal snarl of orgasm. He could hear the squelch of her spasming vagina and actually see the lovejuice bubbling out of her . . .

Working himself viciously, Niall sobbed as the spunk came shooting up from his vitals, then gave a raw broken wail of purest love as Misty fell forward out of her self-induced ecstasy and took the tip of his prick between her jammy reddened lips.

Niall's last conscious thought was that not a single drop of his semen had been spilt.

A small innocuous sound woke him up, and when he opened his eyes, Mary was placing a steaming cup on the table beside his chair.

'Lemon tea,' she said briskly. 'I thought you'd like some. It always bucks me up when I've got a cold.'

Niall shuffled nervously in his seat, looked down, then sighed with relief. His robe was snugly tied and there was no visible sign of what'd most surely been the finest wet dream of his life. It must've been one, he decided, because his body had that absolutely great, all-round warm contented glow it always got from a truly great come.

He was feeling fine, and thinking about trying Mary's cure-all tea, when he saw her bend down – with a smooth and surprising grace – and pick up something from the floor.

Niall's sense of well-being dissolved like Scotch mist, because what Mary was holding and gazing down at with a small sly grin, was a maroon lace glove. She fingered it slowly, and eased it carefully into shape as if she were about to put it on . . .

Still reeling from the glove, Niall took a further blow when she turned slightly, and for the first time since he'd come to, he got a good clear look at her face.

She was still the same not-quite-pretty Mary with the same ugly glasses, yet at the corner of her soft,

205

full and untouched-looking mouth was a smudge
. . . a smudge of bright, brazen flame-red that could
only be lipstick. She caught his look and her eyes
twinkled behind her deceiving spectacles. She
smiled, a new smile that wasn't 'Mary' at all but was
bold, moistly pouting and terrifyingly reminiscent
of . . .

A long supple finger rose and wiped away the
incriminating smudge. She smiled again. The smile
that melted Niall's loins every time he saw it – in
whatever form it took.

'Merry Christmas, Niall,' she purred and slid her
finger wickedly, evocatively and oh-so-familiarly
between her lips.

Not Just a Pretty Face

'I'M NOT JUST a pretty face, you know!'

To be honest, I'm not even one. I'm more what you'd call 'bonny', but Ellis was either too kind or too clever to contradict me.

'Neither am I,' she murmured, not strictly responding to my tipsy rantings. Who cared anyway? She was smiling that smile again, the one that'd driven me mad for three weeks and posed far more questions than it answered.

Three weeks ago Ellis Delaheigh had arrived from the States to take charge of Jackson-Wordsworth Associates, but for me she'd stirred up far more than the management structure! One look at the divine Ellis and my suspicions about myself grew . . .

Was I a lesbian or what?

Ellis was everything I'm not. Tall, lean and vaguely angular, she had the lightfooted grace of a racehorse. All fine bones, fire and arrogance, she'd stride through the office like the Goddess Diana and confound everybody – particularly me! – with her sexy yet touch-me-not air.

Sexuality . . . One of those famous 'grey' areas for me, I'd say.

Although totally un-Ellislike – that's middle-sized, a redhead, and to put it bluntly, busty – I'd always had my fair share of boyfriends – and sex. But for a while – even before Ellis's arrival – I'd been right off men. Well, not completely off them. I'd fancied one or two, but always the same type. Slim, effeminate guys who reminded me of women. And when I'd put my libido on auto and fantasised I'd always dreamed of pulling women. Until the very last minute, that was, when a rather wacky thing seemed to happen. If I was beginning to like the idea of being Sapphic, why did my dreams stop short of the actual sex?

I'd no-one to confide this in, but I knew the moment I set eyes on her that Ellis Delaheigh would understand. She was Razor-woman, cutting right to the heart of things and splitting the true from the false. Yes, before we'd exchanged a single word, Ellis had looked into my eyes and seen my troubled soul.

Speculation about her was rampant. Fuelled by her imperious air it swirled around her like a purple cloak. The men she'd advanced all fancied their chances; and the ones she'd sacked all called her a dyke!

Me, I couldn't work out what she was, except that she was magnificent! And that she'd singled out me – Rosie Warren, visual futurist – for encouragement and promotion. Not before time either! In a boringly traditional ad agency I'd been having trouble with my far-out ideas. But after some split-second decisionmaking, Ellis had pointed her long coral-tipped finger in my buxom direction and said 'This is the Head of Design'!

And here we were celebrating.

I'd nearly died when she'd oh-so-casually

suggested it. Working on a new layout, she'd popped the bland little question. I'd looked up and felt the full force of something I'd never experienced before: sexual interest from another woman. There'd been more in those big, brown, delicately outlined eyes than a night of pasta, vino and shoptalk. Then I'd blushed and blustered . . . and it'd gone again. We'd been back to a simple meal to celebrate my new job.

Entering the restaurant I'd felt like a lummox. Ellis had led the way to our table, her trimly-turned ankles flashing as she walked; her long, flared skirt swirling out around her. Heads had turned and stayed turned. The watchers thinking, no doubt, 'That's class!' Then they'd look at me and think, 'Who's the fat bimbo?'

We'd come straight from the office, and yet Ellis still looked as immaculate as new paint: cool and composed, with not one of her sleek black curls out of place. While I was looking decidedly blowsy . . .

Once, long ago, I'd tried wearing the kind of drapes and ruffles that Ellis always wore, but on me they'd looked wrong. Like someone else's clothes. These days I'd given in and reverted to type. My short, tight suit and clingy cotton top were tarty, but – unfortunately – very me. What was worse my tawny mop was all over the place, and in spite of a good can of body spray liberally distributed, I was smelling embarrassingly musky. That was the 'Ellis Delaheigh' factor; scary as it was, she was arousing me as I'd never been aroused before. I'd nearly fainted in the Ladies when I'd slipped down my pants and discovered the state they were in!

That's why I'd got squiffy on Italian wine and run off at the mouth, singing my own praises as an advertising designer. I know I'd had my suspicions, but juicing up over a member of my own sex was still one helluva shock!

'I'm not just a pretty face, you know.'

'Neither am I.'

'Oh, Ellis, you're beautiful! You're the most beuatiful woman I've ever seen!'

I scowled at my glass, condemning the wine but knowing in my heart I'd've said it all anyway. Even if I'd been on Tizer all night.

'Am I?' asked Ellis softly, her voice like Dietrich. It made my spine melt and my sex throb like a second heartbeat.

'Yes,' I mumbled, feeling like a soppy, lust-addled fool.

'Thank you kindly, Rosie,' she murmured, then fell silently thoughtful for several long, unnerving minutes.

Oh God, no! I'd blown it: gushed and been completely uncool. Watching her toying with her cutlery and looking vaguely troubled, I cringed and waited for one of her effortless, killer-queen put-downs.

Suddenly, she set her fork down with a decisive 'clomp' and looked up and straight into my eyes.

'Okay then, let's go back to my flat and have sex.'

Things went pretty blurry after that, even though I was instantly stone cold sober. I'd got chills and fever now, fears and longings; I wanted Ellis like hell, but what exactly did 'wanting' mean?

What did lesbians do? Should I start or would she? Dodgiest of all: was I actually a lesbian? Would I end up wishing Ellis had a cock? I'd a sneaky feeling I might, but one look at her beautiful face, her soft, smooth skin and her long, graceful body made it seem less important. Well, a bit less . . .

When we got to her flat – a place as subtle and

elegantly expensive-looking as its mistress – all trace of that briefly pensive Ellis had gone.

'Sit down, Rosie.' Her voice was velvet but unyielding and she gestured to a low squashy chair of coffee-coloured leather.

I flopped down like a brainless dolt and just stared at her.

Ellis towered over me in full control. But somewhere in the hauteur, far back in the mix, was a twinge of something far less self-possessed. I couldn't believe it was nerves, but I was in no state for in-depth analysis – especially when she reached down and took the handbag I was clutching so defensively.

'You won't need that,' she said, flinging it into one of the other chairs. Then, closing the space between us, she leaned over me, dug her hand into my hair and pressed her lips hard on to mine.

I nearly fainted again. There was a world of difference between thought and deed, between words and actually making love. I say 'making love' because for me Ellis was too glorious to simply 'have sex' with. Even though she'd called it that herself.

The kiss was long, sweet and thorough, and in spite of everything, felt right. Ellis's tongue was bold; she tasted of wine and fruit, her lips so mobile and delicious it was impossible not to kiss them in return. When our mouths finally parted, she slid gracefully to her knees, then eased her fine kid pumps off her long, slender feet.

But even barefoot and kneeling, Ellis Delaheigh was no supplicant. Not by a long shot!

'Sit back,' she commanded, 'Relax, but don't move.'

I did as I was told: drugged by her perfume, and disorientated by the sight of such a beautiful woman crouched at my feet. Her silky skirt had fanned around her, but it didn't rest there long. Almost before I knew it she was kneeling up over me, peeling my tight jacket off my shoulders and pushing it down. When it wedged at my elbows, my arms were imprisoned. There was a wild look in Ellis's eyes now, and sweat on her upper lip. But she still smelt clean and fresh. She was all flowers, lemon and spices – while I was far less delicate. Sweat and a pungent woman-smell seemed to roll off me in waves.

With my arms pinned I was at her mercy. My cotton top went next; shoved down like my jacket, trapping me even tighter. My breasts jiggled in my lace bra as Ellis arranged me to her liking. I was her raggedy-doll and she was posing me. I was so turned on by this peculiar foreplay it was mortifying. My pants were saturated now, and I imagined a dark, damp patch on the soft leather beneath me . . .

'Let's see what we've got.' She flicked the straps off my shoulders and dragged my bra clear of my breasts. My nipples were standing out like studs, ruby-red against solid blue-veined creaminess. I felt gross and vulgar. Why couldn't I be slim and lean like Ellis?

But I'd never seen Ellis's breasts, had I? Her lushly draped shirts hid even the vaguest hint of their shape.

She liked mine though!

'Lovely!' Her long, cool hands slid under the mounded weight, cupping, lifting and kneading.

I wanted to scream. Ellis's fingers were soft but her grip was firm. She handled my breasts in the rough way I'd always loved. How could she know what I hardly understood myself?

212

Bowing her darkly-curled head, she took a nipple in her mouth and started sucking with all her might. It was like having my tit in a furnace, yet the still, silent observer in my squirming body saw her coral lipstick smear the peak of my breast.

'Ellis,' I groaned as she shifted her mouth to the other nipple and dragged at it like a starving baby. 'Ellis . . . Oh God!' It was as if she'd wound a fine cord around my clitoris and threaded it out through my tortured breasts. Every suck went directly to my swimming crotch.

'Easy, baby, easy!' she soothed, her mouth full of nipple, then drew back, dropping a kiss on my wet breast.

'Okay, let's see your snatch!' The words were coarse, and her American twang more pronounced now, but to me it was the Song of Solomon. Deftly, with an expression of intense concentration, she pushed up my skirt then gripped my tights and panties in one bunch and hauled them down to my ankles. 'Spread your legs, baby,' she whispered.

For almost a minute, she studied my naked sex, and behind my eyes, I saw what she saw: a page from a porno mag; an arrangement of skin and cheap clothes that was far more obscene than simple nudity . . .

Its very crudeness was uplifting. I was a sacrifice to the divine Ellis, and my breasts and sex had a life of their own, a voice to sing the praises of the woman who bent before me.

She lapped sweat from the crease of my groin. She kissed my belly, my thighs, my fuzzy mound; even my tight-less knees. The clever witch kissed everywhere but the tiny piece of flesh that needed it most . . .

Desperation snuffed out my torpor.

'My clit, for God's sake,' I croaked. 'Suck my clit, you bitch!'

I'd called my boss a 'bitch' and told, no, ordered her to suck me off. But I was beyond caring now . . . Only my clit mattered. It felt huge and swollen, protruding, caught in a beam of hard light.

In a slow motion movement, Ellis leant forward and obeyed me. Her soft hair fell across my thighs as she clamped her lips around me. Then I was screaming, writhing, coming . . . pumping my hips against her as my hole pulsed like a sea creature sucking in life. It was gorgeous, tormenting, celestial, and I didn't give a damn if Ellis was a woman, I adored her!

I lay half-stupefied for God knows how long, with Ellis's warm face resting on my thigh. When at last she looked up and roused me, her voice had a faintly tentative note. 'Why don't you take a shower, honey? Then we'll go to bed – maybe?'

Confused, and tugging at my clothes, I escaped to the bathroom, and presently, slid naked into Ellis's wide cream-sheeted bed, as she in turn took a shower.

What Ellis had done had been special and beautiful, but now I was hating myself for my doubts. In spite of her unorthodox methods, she'd been tender and supremely giving. She'd made me come; transformed me. But could I do the same for her? Could I touch and kiss another woman's body? A body I still hadn't seen . . . She'd gone into the bathroom fully clothed, with a heavy silk kimono over her arm.

'You're not sure, are you?'

I must've nodded off, tired out by it all, because I'd never even heard her return.

Ellis slid into bed beside me, still swathed in her

214

exquisite kimono, and in the subdued light, I gazed at her.

Bare of her make-up, she looked younger somehow, and prettier. Yet though still my beautiful Ellis – with her clear dewy skin, and her hair damp from the shower – she seemed discreetly difference, in a way I couldn't put my finger on . . .

I shuddered.

'What's wrong, honey?' she said, her voice alive with a strange edginess.

'I . . . You . . . You're right, Ellis, I'm not sure. I'm not sure of anything,' I muttered, feeling mean and small, 'This'll sound stupid, but . . . but . . . Oh God, Ellis,' I wailed, 'I don't know if I'm a lesbian or not!'

Then suddenly she was laughing: an odd deep sort of laugh that sounded nervous yet relieved, 'Come here, sweetheart, let's see if we can make up our minds.'

'*Our* minds? What do you mean, make up *our* minds?'

'The thing is, Rosie, I'm not sure what *I* am either.' She kissed me then, just once, on the lips, then gently but insistently pushed my hand inside her kimono. Holding my fingers in hers, she slid them down over a hard, flat belly and crisp, springy hair, then closed them around what lay below.

It was a full thirty seconds before it dawned on me what I was holding.

A cock! A warm, stiff, velvety cock!

'Oh God, you're a man!' I cried, instinctively stroking the evidence.

'Yeah, I suppose I am . . . sort of,' he murmured, more vulnerable in that moment than *I'd* ever been, 'Does it bother you?'

I thought about it for a tenth of a second, then shazam! A fatal blow to heart, brain and sex. The grey areas weren't grey any more, and the divine Ellis was still divine.

'No, not in the slightest,' I whispered, smiling. 'So let's get on with it, shall we?'

And with that, I moved over his slim brown body and did all the dirty, daring, delicious things to it that suddenly came so naturally.

And why not? He *is* the woman I love!